**"I have a son. *We* have a son. He will be four years old in a little less than three months."**

He gaped at her in shock, and for several long seconds the silence was heavy between them. She wished she could read his mind and know what he was thinking.

"A son?" he echoed in disbelief.

"His name is Tomas. I named him after you."

During the night they'd shared Miguel had confided that Tomas was his middle name. And his father's name.

Miguel dragged a hand down his face as if still hardly able to comprehend what she was saying. "I don't understand. How did this happen? We used protection."

She batted down the flicker of anger. Hadn't she asked herself the same question while staring down at the positive pregnancy test? But having him think, even for a moment, that she might have done this on purpose made her grind her teeth in frustration.

"Protection can fail, Miguel. I'm sorry to spring this on you so suddenly. You need to know I tried to find you after you left. I called your cell phone and searched for you on all the popular social media websites. When I couldn't find you I assumed you were working somewhere remote with Doctors Without Borders, following your dream." She spread her hands wide. "I didn't know Seville was your home. Had no way of knowing you were here all this time."

Miguel looked shell-shocked as he lowered himself slowly onto a kitchen chair. "A son. Tomas. I can barely comprehend what you are telling me."

**Dear Reader**

Like many of you I've spent years as an armchair traveller, learning about other countries and other cultures by reading rather than visiting.

Last year I had the tremendous opportunity to visit Seville (pronounced Sevilla) in Spain. My family and I had a great time, and when I returned home I had this story whirling around in my head about how an American woman falls in love with a Spanish surgeon.

Miguel and Kat originally meet in the US, when Miguel is an exchange student, but when they meet again Kat is visiting Miguel's home city of Seville. Sparks flash and the passion that they shared once before returns in force. But can they create a life together coming from such different cultures? Will true love conquer all?

I hope you enjoy reading Miguel and Kat's story as much as I enjoyed writing it. Don't hesitate to visit my website or find me on Facebook—I love to hear from my readers.

Sincerely

*Laura Iding*

www.lauraiding.com

# HER LITTLE
# SPANISH SECRET

BY
LAURA IDING

First published in Great Britain 2012
by Mills & Boon, an imprint of Harlequin (UK) Limited.
Harlequin (UK) Limited, Eton House, 18-24 Paradise Road,
Richmond, Surrey TW9 1SR

© Laura Iding  2012

ISBN: 978 0 263 22900 4

**Laura Iding** loved reading as a child, and when she ran out of books she readily made up her own, completing a little detective mini-series when she was twelve. But, despite her aspirations for being an author, her parents insisted she look into a 'real' career. So the summer after she turned thirteen she volunteered as a Candy Striper, and fell in love with nursing. Now, after twenty years of experience in trauma/critical care, she's thrilled to combine her career and her hobby into one—writing Medical Romances™ for Mills & Boon. Laura lives in the northern part of the United States, and spends all her spare time with her two teenage kids (help!)—a daughter and a son—and her husband. Enjoy!

### Recent titles by Laura Iding:

DATING DR DELICIOUS
A KNIGHT FOR NURSE HART
THE NURSE'S BROODING BOSS
THE SURGEON'S NEW YEAR WEDDING WISH
EXPECTING A CHRISTMAS MIRACLE

**These books are also available in eBook format
from www.millsandboon.co.uk**

This book is dedicated to the Milwaukee WisRWA group.
Thanks to all of you for your ongoing support.

# PROLOGUE

*Four and a half years earlier...*

K AT had never seen so much blood—it pooled on the floor and stained the walls of the O.R. suite. Dr. Miguel Vasquez, along with two other trauma surgeons, had worked as hard as they could to stop the bleeding but to no avail. Their young, pregnant patient and her unborn baby had died.

After the poor woman's body had been sent to the morgue, Kat was left alone to finish putting the supplies and equipment away while the housekeepers cleaned up the blood. Only once they were finished did she head over to the staff locker room. Thankfully, her shift was over, she was exhausted. Yet as tired as she was physically, she was emotionally keyed up, and couldn't get the horrific scene from the O.R. out of her mind. They hadn't had a case like that in a long time.

After she changed out of her scrubs into a pair of well-worn jeans and a short-sleeved sweater, she found Dr. Vasquez sitting in the staff lounge, holding his head in his hands. He looked so upset and dejected that she stopped—unable to simply walk away.

"Please don't torture yourself over this," she urged

softly, as she sank down beside him on the sofa close enough that their shoulders brushed. "Her death wasn't your fault."

Miguel slowly lifted and turned his head to look at her, his eyes full of agony. "I should have called the rest of the team in earlier."

"You called them as soon as you discovered her abdomen was full of blood and they came as soon as they could," she corrected. "No one knew she was pregnant, it was too early to tell."

"I should have examined her more closely down in the trauma bay," he muttered, more to himself than to her. "Then we would have known."

"Do you really think that would have made a difference?" she asked softly. "Even if the other two surgeons had been notified earlier, they wouldn't have been able to come right away. Dr. Baccus said they were resuscitating a patient in the I.C.U. All of us in the O.R. suite did the best we could."

He stared at her for a long moment, and then sighed. "I can't help thinking about what I should have done differently. I know we can't save every patient, but she was just so young. And pregnant. I can't help feeling I failed her."

She put her hand on his arm, trying to offer some reassurance. "If three of the best trauma surgeons in the whole hospital couldn't save her or her baby, then it wasn't meant to be."

A ghost of a smile played along the edges of his mouth, and she was glad she'd been able to make him feel a little better. Because what she'd said was true. Everyone talked about Miguel's skill in the O.R. He could have stayed here in the U.S. once his fellowship was finished, even though he'd made it clear that wasn't part of his plan.

She reluctantly slid her hand from his arm and rose to her feet. But she'd only taken two steps when he stopped her.

"Katerina?"

She hesitated and turned to look back at him, surprised and secretly pleased he'd remembered her first name. They'd operated on dozens of patients together, but while she'd always been keenly aware of Miguel, she had never been absolutely sure he'd noticed her the same way. "Yes?"

"Do you have plans for tonight? If not, would you join me? We could get a bite to eat or something."

She wasn't hungry, but could tell Miguel didn't want to be alone, and suddenly she didn't either. Word amongst the O.R. staff was that Miguel wasn't in the market for a relationship since his time in the U.S. was limited, but she ignored the tiny warning flickering in the back of her mind. "I don't have any plans for tonight, and I'd love to have dinner." *Or something.*

*"Muy bien."* He rose to his feet and held out his hand. She took it and suppressed a shiver when a tingle of awareness shot up her arm.

But she didn't pull away. Instead, she stayed close at his side while they left the hospital together.

# CHAPTER ONE

"Down, Mama. *Down!*"

"Soon, Tommy. I promise." Katerina Richardson fought a wave of exhaustion and tightened her grip on her wriggly son. She couldn't imagine anything more torturous than being stuck in a plane for sixteen hours with an active soon-to-be four-year-old. She didn't even want to think of the longer flight time on the return trip.

Plenty of time to worry about that, later. For now they'd finally arrived in Seville, Spain. And she desperately needed to get to the hospital to see how her half sister was doing after being hit by a car. The information from Susan Horton, the coordinator for the study abroad program, had been sketchy at best.

"I can't believe the stupid airline lost my luggage," her best friend, Diana Baylor, moaned as they made their way out of the airport to the line of people waiting for taxis. "It's so hot here in April compared to Cambridge, Massachusetts. I'm already sweating—I can't imagine staying in these same clothes for very long."

Kat felt bad for her friend, who'd only come on this trip in the first place as a favor to her, but what could she do? Diana's lost luggage was the least of her concerns. "Don't worry, I'll share my stuff or we'll buy what you need."

"Down, Mama. Down!" Tommy's tone, accompanied by his wiggling, became more insistent.

"Okay, but you have to hold my hand," Kat warned her son, as she put him on his feet. She'd let him run around in the baggage claim area while they'd waited for their luggage, but even that hadn't put a dent in his energy level. She was grateful he'd slept on the plane, even though she hadn't. Kat grabbed hold of his hand before he could make a beeline for the road. "Stay next to me, Tommy."

He tugged on her hand, trying to go in the opposite direction from where they needed to wait for a taxi. Thank heavens the line was moving fast. Her son was as dark as she was blonde and if she had a nickel for every person who'd asked her if he was adopted, she'd be rich. Even here, she could feel curious eyes on them.

"No, Tommy. This way. Look, a car! We're going to go for a ride!"

His attention diverted, Tommy readily climbed into the cab after Diana. They all squished into the back seat for the short ride to their hotel. "Hesperia Hotel, please," she told the taxi driver.

"Hesperia? *No comprendo* Hesperia." Their cab driver shook his head as he pulled out into traffic, waving his hand rather impatiently. *"No comprendo."*

Kat refused to panic and quickly rummaged through her carry-on bag to pull out the hotel confirmation document. She handed it to him so he could read the name of the hotel for himself. He looked at the paper and made a sound of disgust. "Es-peer-ria," he said, emphasizing the Spanish pronunciation. "Esperia Hotel."

Properly chastised, she belatedly remembered from her two years of high-school Spanish that the H was silent. Being in Spain brought back bittersweet memories of Tommy's father, especially during their three-hour layover in Madrid. She'd briefly toyed with the thought of trying to find Miguel, but had then realized her idea was ludicrous. Madrid was a huge city and she had no idea where to even start, if he'd even be there, which she seriously doubted. He may have studied there but it was possible he'd moved on. "*Sí*. Hesperia Hotel, *gracias*."

The taxi driver mumbled something unintelligible and probably uncomplimentary in Spanish, under his breath. Kat ignored him.

"Are you going to the hospital today?" Diana asked with a wide yawn. "I'm voting for a nap first."

"I doubt Tommy will sleep any time soon," she reminded her friend. "And, yes, I'm going to head to the hospital as soon as we get the hotel room secured. I'm sorry, but you'll have to watch Tommy for a while."

"I know," Diana said quickly. "I don't mind." Kat knew Diana wouldn't renege on her duties, seeing as Kat had been the one to pay for her friend's airfare, along with footing the hotel bill. Kat hadn't minded as she'd needed someone to help watch over her son. "Wow, Kat, take a look at the architecture of that building over there. Isn't it amazing?"

"Yeah, amazing." Kat forced a smile, because Diana was right—the view was spectacular. Yet the thrill of being in Europe for the first time in her life couldn't make her forget the reason they were there. The knot in her stomach tightened as she wondered what she'd discover when she went to the hospital. Susan Horton, the director of the study abroad program at Seville University, had called just thirty-six hours ago, to let her know that her younger half sister, Juliet, had a serious head injury and was too sick to be flown back to the U.S. for care.

Kat had immediately made arrangements to fly over to Seville in order to be there for her sister.

She and Juliet hadn't been particularly close. And not just because of the seven-year age gap. They had different fathers and for some reason Juliet had always seemed to resent Kat. Their respective fathers had both abandoned their mother, which should have given them something in common. After their mother had been diagnosed with pancreatic cancer, Kat had promised her mother she'd look after Juliet.

Juliet had gone a little wild after their mother's death, but had settled down somewhat after she'd finished her second year of college. At the ripe old age of twenty-one, Juliet had insisted on studying abroad for the spring semester of her junior year. Kat had been forced to pick up a lot of call weekends in order to pay for the program, but she'd managed. To be fair, Juliet had come up with a good portion of the money herself.

Kat felt guilty now about how she'd been secretly relieved to put her younger sister on a plane to Spain. But even if she'd tried to talk Juliet out of going, it wouldn't have worked. Juliet would only have resented her even more.

How had the accident happened? All she'd been told

was that Juliet had run out into the street and had been hit by a car, but she didn't know anything further.

Getting to the hotel didn't take long, although there was another hassle as she figured out the dollar to Euro exchange in order to pay the cranky cab driver. As soon as Diana and Tommy were settled in the hotel room, Kat asked the front-desk clerk for directions to the hospital. She managed to figure out how to get there on the metro, which wasn't very different than using the subway back home.

Seville's teaching hospital was larger than she'd expected and that gave her hope that Juliet was getting good medical and nursing care. Kat found her sister in their I.C.U and walked in, only to stop abruptly when she saw Juliet was connected to a ventilator. Her stomach clenched even harder when she noted several dark bruises and small lacerations marring her sister's pale skin.

"Dear heaven," she breathed, trailing her gaze from her sister up to the heart monitor. She'd done a year-long stint in the I.C.U before going to the O.R. so she'd known what to expect, but had hoped that Juliet might have improved during the time it had taken her to make the travel arrangements and actually arrive in Seville.

A nurse, dressed head to toe in white, complete with nurse's cap on her dark hair, came into the room behind her. Kat blinked back tears and turned to the nurse. "How is she? Has her condition improved? What is the extent of her injury? Can I speak to the doctor?"

The nurse stared at her blankly for a moment and then began talking in rapid Spanish, none of which Kat could understand.

Kat wanted to cry. She desperately paged through the English/Spanish dictionary she held, trying to look up words in Spanish to explain what she wanted to know. *"¿Donde esta el doctor? ¿Habla Ingles?"* she finally asked. Where is the doctor? Speak English?

The nurse spun around and left the room.

Kat sank into a chair next to Juliet's bed, gently clasping her half sister's hand in hers. Maybe the age difference, and completely opposite personalities, had kept them from being close, but Juliet was still her sister. With their mother gone, they only had each other.

She had to believe Juliet would pull through this. Her sister was young and strong, surely she'd be fine.

Kat put her head down on the edge of Juliet's bed, closing her eyes just for a moment, trying to combat the deep fatigue of jet lag and her fear regarding the seriousness of her sister's injuries.

She didn't think she'd fallen asleep, but couldn't be sure how much time had passed when she heard a deep male voice, thankfully speaking in English. She lifted her head and prised her heavy eyelids open.

"I understand you have questions regarding the condition of Juliet Campbell?"

"Yes, thank you." She quickly rose to her feet and blinked the grit from her eyes as she turned to face the doctor.

His familiar facial features made the room gyrate wildly, and she had to grasp the edge of her sister's side rail for support. "Miguel?" she whispered in shock, wondering if she was dreaming. Had thoughts of Tommy's father conjured up a mirage? Or was it just the doctor's Hispanic features, dark hair falling rakishly over his forehead, deep brown eyes gazing into hers, that were so achingly familiar?

"Katerina." His eyes widened in surprise, and she couldn't help feeling relieved to know she wasn't the only one knocked off balance at this chance meeting. For several long seconds they simply stared at each other across the room. Slowly, he smiled, relieving part of the awkwardness. "What a pleasant surprise to see you again. How are you?"

She tightened her grip on the bed rail behind her because her knees threatened to give away. "I'm fine, thanks." She struggled to keep her tone friendly, even though for one beautiful night they'd been far more than just friends. Yet despite her fanciful thoughts during the Madrid layover, she hadn't really expected to see Miguel again.

He looked good. Better than good. Miguel was taller than most Latino men, with broad shoulders and a golden skin tone that showcased his bright smile. His dark eyes were mesmerizing. If not for his full name, Dr. Miguel Vasquez, embroidered on his white lab coat—she'd for sure think this was a dream.

She knew Juliet's condition needed to be her primary concern, but she had so many other questions she wanted to ask him. "I'm surprised to find you here in Seville. I thought you lived in Madrid?"

He didn't answer right away, and she thought she saw a flash of guilt shadow his dark eyes. She glanced away, embarrassed. She didn't want him feeling guilty for the night they'd shared together. Or for leaving so abruptly when notified of his father's illness. It wasn't as if they'd been dating or anything.

Neither was it his fault she'd let her feelings spin out of control that night.

When she'd discovered she was pregnant, she'd called his cell phone, the only number she'd had, but the number had already been out of service. She'd assumed he hadn't kept his old American phone once he'd returned to Spain. She'd looked for him on several social media sites, but hadn't found him. After about six months she'd stopped trying.

"I live here," he said simply. "My family's olive farm is just twenty minutes outside Seville."

"I see," she said, although she really didn't. Obviously, she hadn't known much about Miguel's family. She could hardly picture him growing up on an olive farm. She'd simply assumed because he was a Madrid exchange student that he'd lived there. She forced a smile, wishing they could recapture the easy camaraderie they'd once shared. "How's your father?"

"He passed away three and a half years ago." The shadows in Miguel's eyes betrayed his grief.

"I'm sorry," she murmured helplessly. She'd known that Miguel had needed to return to Spain when his father had been sick, but she was a little surprised that he'd stayed here, even after his father had passed away.

During the night they'd shared together he'd confided about how he dreamed of joining Doctors Without Borders. When she hadn't been able to get in touch with Miguel once she'd discovered she was pregnant, she'd imagined him working in some distant country.

Why hadn't he followed his dream? He'd told her about how he was only waiting to be finished with his family obligations. And his father had passed away three and a half years ago. He should have been long gone by now.

Not that Miguel's choices were any of her business.

Except, now that he was here, how was she going to tell him about their son?

Panic soared, squeezing the air from her lungs. She struggled to take a deep breath, trying to calm her jagged nerves. Right now she needed to focus on her sister. She pulled herself together with an effort. "Will you please tell me about Juliet's head injury? How bad is it? What exactly is her neuro status?"

"Your sister's condition is serious, but stable. She responds to pain now, which she wasn't doing at first. She does have a subarachnoid hemorrhage that we are monitoring very closely."

A subarachnoid hemorrhage wasn't good news, but she'd been prepared for that. "Is she following commands?" Kat asked.

"Not yet, but she's young, Katerina. She has a good chance of getting through this."

She gave a tight nod, wanting to believe him. "I know. I'm hopeful that she'll wake up soon."

"Katerina, I have to get to surgery as I have a patient waiting, but I would like to see you again. Would you please join me for dinner tonight? Say around eight-thirty or nine?"

She blinked in surprise and tried to think of a graceful way out of the invitation. She knew he was asking her out from some sense of obligation, because they'd spent one intense night together.

But she needed time to get the fog of fatigue out of her mind. Time to think about if and when to share

the news about Tommy. Obviously Miguel deserved to
know the truth, but what about Tommy? Did he deserve
a father who didn't want him? A father who'd made it
clear he wasn't looking for a family?

She didn't know what to do.

"I'm sorry, but I'm sure I'll be asleep by then," she
murmured, averting her gaze to look at her sister. "I
just flew in today and I'm a bit jet-lagged."

She steeled herself against the flash of disappointment in his eyes. Juliet's well-being came first. And
Tommy's was a close second.

As far as she was concerned, Miguel Vasquez would
just have to wait.

Miguel couldn't believe Katerina Richardson was actually here, in Seville.

He allowed his gaze to roam over her, branding her
image on his mind. She wasn't beautiful in the classi-
cal sense, but he'd always found her attractive with her
peaches and cream complexion and long golden blonde
hair that she normally wore in a ponytail. Except for
that one night, when he'd run his fingers through the
silk tresses.

To this day he couldn't explain why he'd broken his
cardinal rule by asking her out. Granted, he'd been dev-
astated over losing their patient, but he'd been determined to avoid emotional entanglements, knowing he
was leaving when the year was up. He knew better than
to let down his guard, but he'd been very attracted to
Katerina and had suspected the feeling was mutual.
That night he'd given up his fight to stay away.

But then the news about his father's stroke had pulled

him from Katerina's bed the next morning. He'd rushed home to Seville. His father's condition had been worse than he'd imagined, and his father had ultimately died twelve painful months later. His mother was already gone, and during his father's illness his younger brother, Luis, had started drinking. Miguel had been forced to put his own dreams on hold to take over the olive farm, which had been in the Vasquez family for generations, until he could get Luis sobered up.

His visceral reaction to seeing Katerina again stunned him. He hadn't allowed himself to miss her. Besides, he only had three months left on his contract here at the hospital and he'd be finally free to join Doctors Without Borders.

And this time,nothing was going to stop him. Not his brother Luis. And certainly not Katerina.

He shook off his thoughts with an effort. Logically he knew he should accept her excuse, but he found himself pressing the issue. "Maybe a light meal after siesta, then? Certainly you have to eat some time."

There was a wariness reflected in her green eyes that hadn't been there in the past. He wondered what had changed in the four and a half years they'd been apart. He was relieved to note she wasn't wearing a wedding ring even though her personal life wasn't any of his business. He couldn't allow himself to succumb to Katerina's spell—he refused to make the same mistakes his father had.

"You've described my sister's head injury, but is there anything else? Other injuries I need to be aware of?" she asked, changing the subject.

He dragged his attention to his patient. "Juliet was

hit on the right side. Her right leg is broken in two places and we had to operate to get the bones aligned properly. She has several rib fractures and some internal bleeding that appears to be resolving. Her head injury is the greatest of our concerns. Up until late yesterday she wasn't responding at all, even to pain. The fact that there is some response now gives us hope she may recover."

Katerina's pale skin blanched even more, and his gut clenched when he noted the tears shimmering in her bright green eyes. They reminded him, too much, about the night they'd shared. An intense, intimate, magical night that had ended abruptly with his brother's phone call about their father. She'd cried for him when he'd been unable to cry for himself.

"When can she be transported back to the United States?" she asked.

The instinctive protest at the thought of her leaving surprised him. What was wrong with him? He wrestled his emotions under control. "Not until I'm convinced her neurological status has truly stabilized," he reluctantly admitted.

Katerina nodded, as if she'd expected that response. "Are you my sister's doctor? Or just one of the doctors here who happen to speak English?" she asked. Her gaze avoided his, staying at the level of his chest.

"Yes, I'm your sister's doctor. As you know, I'm a surgeon who does both general and trauma surgery cases."

"Do any of the nurses speak English?"

Seville didn't have the same tourist draw as Madrid or Barcelona, which meant not as many of the locals spoke English. Miguel had originally learned English from his American mother, who'd taught him before she'd died. He'd learned even more English during his time at the University of Madrid. In fact, he'd earned the opportunity to live and study medicine in the U.S. at Harvard University.

There he'd ultimately become a doctor. And met Katerina. He dragged his thoughts out of the past. "No, the nurses don't speak much English, I'm afraid."

She closed her eyes and rubbed her temples, as if she had a pounding headache. Once again he found himself on the verge of offering comfort. But he didn't dare, no matter how much he wanted to.

"I would appreciate periodic updates on my sister's condition whenever you have time to spare from the rest of your patients," she said finally.

The way she turned her back on him, as if to dismiss him, made him scowl. He wanted to demand she look at him, talk to him, but of course there wasn't time. Glancing at his watch only confirmed he was already late for his scheduled surgery. "I'd be happy to give you an update later today, if you have time at, say, four o'clock?" He purposefully gave her the same time he normally ate a late lunch, right after siesta.

She spun around to face him. "But—" She stopped herself and then abruptly nodded. "Of course. Four o'clock would be fine."

He understood she'd only agreed to see him so that she could get updates on her sister, but that didn't stop him from being glad he'd gotten his way on this. "I look forward to seeing you later, then, Katerina," he said softly.

He could barely hide the thrill of anticipation racing through him, knowing he'd see her again soon, as he hurried down to the operating room.

## CHAPTER TWO

"So what do you think? Do I really need to tell Miguel about Tommy?" Kat asked, after she'd caught up with Diana and Tommy at the park located right across the street from their hotel. The park was next to a school and seeing all the kids in their navy blue and white uniforms playing on the playground wasn't so different from the preschool Tommy attended back in the U.S.

"I don't think you should do anything yet," Diana advised. "I mean, what do we know about the custody laws in Spain? What if Miguel has the right to take Tommy away from you?"

The very thought made her feel sick to her stomach. "Tommy is a U.S. citizen," she pointed out, striving for logic. "That has to count for something."

"Maybe, maybe not. I don't think you should say anything until we know what we're dealing with. Miguel is a big important doctor at the largest hospital here. Maybe he has connections, friends in high places? I think you need to understand exactly what you're dealing with if you tell him."

Kat sighed, and rubbed her temples, trying to ease the ache. Lack of sleep, worry over Juliet and now seeing Miguel again had all combined into one giant, pounding headache. "And how are we going to find out the child custody laws here? Neither one of us can speak Spanish, so it's not like we can just look up the information on the internet."

"We could check with the American Embassy," Diana said stubbornly.

"I suppose. Except that seems like a lot of work when I'm not even sure Miguel will bother to fight me for Tommy. During our night together he told me his dream was to join Doctors Without Borders. He made it clear he wanted the freedom to travel, not settling down in one place."

"Except here he is in Seville four and a half years later," Diana pointed out reasonably. "Maybe he's changed his mind about his dream?"

"Maybe." She couldn't argue Diana's point. She still found it hard to wrap her mind around the fact that Miguel was here, in Seville. She'd stayed with her sister for another hour or so after he'd left, slightly reassured that Juliet's condition was indeed stable, before she'd come back to the hotel to unpack her things. Seeing Miguel had made her suddenly anxious to find her son.

Tommy was having a great time running around in the park, chasing butterflies. As she watched him, the physical similarities seemed even more acute. She realized the minute Miguel saw Tommy, he'd know the truth without even needing to be told.

Although Miguel wouldn't have to see him, a tiny voice in the back of her mind reminded her. Tommy could stay here with Diana and in a couple of days hopefully Juliet would be stable enough to be sent back to the U.S. Miguel didn't need to know anything about their son.

As soon as the thought formed, she felt a sense of shame. Keeping Tommy's presence a secret would be taking the coward's way out. Diana was worried about the Spanish custody laws, but Kat had other reasons for not wanting to tell Miguel about Tommy. Being intimate with Miguel had touched her in a way she hadn't expected. When she'd discovered she was pregnant, she'd been torn between feeling worried at how she'd manage all alone to secretly thrilled to have a part of Miguel growing inside her.

She knew he hadn't felt the same way about her. Men had sex with women all the time, and lust certainly wasn't love. She knew better than to get emotionally involved. In her experience men didn't remain faithful or stick around for the long haul. Especially when there was the responsibility of raising children. Her father and Juliet's father had proven that fact.

She gave Miguel credit for being upfront and honest about his inability to stay. He hadn't lied to her, hadn't told her what he'd thought she'd wanted to hear. It was her fault for not doing a better job of protecting her heart.

Telling Miguel about Tommy opened up the possibility that she'd have to see Miguel on a regular basis. If they were raising a child together, there would be no way to avoid him. She would have to hide her true feelings every time they were together.

Unless Miguel still didn't want the responsibility of a son? There was a part of her that really hoped so, because then he wouldn't insist on joint custody.

Now she was getting way ahead of herself. Maybe she could tell Miguel about Tommy and reassure him that she didn't need help, financially or otherwise, to raise her son. She and Tommy would be fine on their own. The way they had been for nearly four years.

"Don't agonize over this, Kat. You don't have to tell him this minute, we just got here. Give me a little time to do some research first, okay?"

"I guess," she agreed doubtfully. Diana was clearly concerned, but she was confident that Tommy had rights as an American citizen. "I won't do anything right away, although I really think I'm going to have to tell him eventually. I tried to call him when I discovered I was pregnant, even tried to find him on all the popular social media websites. Now that I know he's here, I need to be honest with him."

"Then why do you look like you're about to cry?" Diana asked.

"Because I'm scared," she murmured, trying to sniffle back her tears. "I couldn't bear it if Miguel tried to fight for custody."

"Okay, let's just say that the Spanish law is the same as the U.S. regarding joint custody. You mentioned he wasn't wearing a wedding ring, but we both know that doesn't always mean much. Miguel might be married or seriously involved in a relationship. Could be the last thing on earth that he wants is to fight for joint custody."

"You're right," she agreed, even though the thought of Miguel being married or involved with someone didn't make her feel any better. "Okay, I need to get a grip. Maybe I'll try talking to Miguel first, try to find out about his personal life before springing the news on him."

Diana nodded eagerly. "Good idea. Meanwhile, I'll see if I can call the U.S. embassy to get more information."

Kat nodded, even though deep down she knew she'd have to tell him. Because Miguel deserved to know. Besides at some point Tommy was going to ask about his father. She refused to lie to her son.

The spear in her heart twisted painfully and tears pricked her eyes. As difficult as it was to be a single mother, she couldn't bear the thought of sending Tommy off to be with his father in a far-away country. Although she knew she could come with Tommy, no matter how difficult it would be to see Miguel again.

If Miguel was truly planning to join Doctors Without Borders, maybe all of this worry would be for nothing. She and Tommy would go back home and continue living their lives.

Tommy tripped and fell, and she leaped off the park bench and rushed over, picking him up and lavishing him with kisses before he could wail too loudly. "There, now, you're okay, big guy."

"Hurts," he sniffed, rubbing his hands over his eyes and smearing dirt all over his face.

"I know, but Mommy will kiss it all better." Holding her son close, nuzzling his neck, she desperately hoped Miguel would be honorable enough to do what was best for Tommy.

Kat returned to the hotel room to change her clothes and freshen up a bit before going back to the hospital to see

Juliet and Miguel. She'd left Diana and Tommy at the local drugstore, picking out a few necessities for Diana to hold her over until her luggage arrived. They'd also picked up two prepaid disposable phones, so they could keep in touch with each other. After fifteen minutes, and with the help of one shopkeeper who did speak a bit of English, they had the phones activated and working.

The metro was far more crowded towards the end of the workday, forcing her to stand, clinging to the overhead pole.

At her stop, she got off the cramped carriage and walked the short distance to the hospital. The temperature had to be pushing eighty and by the time she arrived, she was hot and sweaty again.

So much for her attempt to look nice for Miguel.

Ridiculous to care one way or the other how she looked. Men weren't exactly knocking down her door, especially once they realized she had a son. Not that she was interested in dating.

She hadn't been with anyone since spending the night with Miguel. At first because she'd been pregnant and then because being a single mother was all-consuming. But she didn't regret a single minute of having Tommy.

In the hospital, she went up to the I.C.U. and paused outside Juliet's doorway, relieved to discover Miguel wasn't there, waiting for her. Her sister had been turned so that she was lying on her right side facing the doorway, but otherwise her condition appeared unchanged.

She crossed over and took Juliet's hand in hers. "Hi, Jules, I'm back. Can you hear me? Squeeze my hand if you can hear me."

Juliet's hand didn't move within hers.

"Wiggle your toes. Can you wiggle your toes for me?"

Juliet's non-broken leg moved, but Kat couldn't figure out if the movement had been made on purpose or not. When she asked a second time, the leg didn't move, so she assumed the latter.

She pulled up a chair and sat down beside her sister, glancing curiously at the chart hanging off the end of the bed. She didn't bother trying to read it, as it would all be in Spanish, but she wished she could read the medical information for herself, to see how Juliet was progressing.

She kept up her one-sided conversation with her sister for the next fifteen minutes or so. Until she ran out of things to say.

"Katerina?"

The way Miguel said her name brought back a fresh wave of erotic memories of their night together and she tried hard to paste a *friendly* smile on her face, before rising to her feet and facing him. "Hello, Miguel. How did your surgery go this morning?"

"Very well, thanks. Would you mind going across the street to the restaurant to talk?" he asked. "I've missed lunch."

She instinctively wanted to say no, but that seemed foolish and petty so she nodded. She glanced back at her sister, leaning over the side rail to talk to her. "I love you, sis. See you soon," she said, before moving away to meet Miguel in the doorway.

As they walked down the stairs to the main level of the hospital, he handed her a stack of papers. "I spent some time translating bits of Juliet's chart for you, so that you can get a sense as to how she's doing."

Her jaw dropped in surprise and for a moment she couldn't speak, deeply touched by his kind consideration. "Thank you," she finally murmured, taking the paperwork he offered. Miguel had often been thoughtful of others and she was glad he hadn't changed during the time they's spent apart. She couldn't imagine where he'd found the time to translate her sister's chart for her between seeing patients and doing surgery, but she was extremely grateful for his efforts.

He put his hand on the small of her back, guiding her towards the restaurant across the street from the hospital. The warmth of his hand seemed to burn through her thin cotton blouse, branding her skin. She was keenly aware of him, his scent wreaking havoc with her concentration, as they made their way across the street. There was outdoor seating beneath cheerful red and white umbrellas and she gratefully sat in the shade, putting the table between them.

The waiter came over and the two men conversed in rapid-fire Spanish. She caught maybe one familiar word out of a dozen.

"What would you like to drink, Katerina?" Miguel asked. "Beer? Wine? Soft drink?"

"You ordered a soft drink, didn't you?" she asked.

He flashed a bright smile and nodded. "You remember some Spanish, no?" he asked with clear approval.

"Yes, *muy poco*, very little," she agreed. "I'll have the same, please."

Miguel ordered several *tapas*, the Spanish form of appetizers, along with their soft drinks. When the food arrived, she had no idea what she was eating, but whatever it was it tasted delicious.

"Do you want to review Juliet's chart now?" he asked. "I can wait and answer your questions."

"I'll read it later, just tell me what you know." She wanted to hear from him first. Besides, there was no way she'd be able to concentrate on her sister's chart with him sitting directly across from her.

He took his time, sipping his drink, before answering. "Juliet has begun moving around more, which is a good sign. She will likely start to intermittently follow commands soon. We have done a CT scan of her brain earlier this morning and the area of bleeding appears to be resolving slowly."

She nodded, eating another of the delicious *tapas* on the plate between them. There were olives too, and she wondered if they were from Miguel's family farm. "I'm glad. I guess all we can do right now is wait and see."

"True," he agreed. He helped himself to more food as well. "Katerina, how is your mother doing? Wasn't she scheduled to have surgery right before I left the States?"

She nodded, her appetite fading. "Yes. The result of her surgery showed stage-four pancreatic cancer. She died a couple months later." Despite the fear of being a single mother, at the time of her mother's passing, her pregnancy had been one of the few bright spots in her life. Things had been difficult until Juliet had gone off to college. Thankfully, her friend Diana had been there for her, even offering to be her labor coach.

"I'm sorry," he murmured, reaching across the table to capture her hand in his. "We both lost our parents about the same time, didn't we?"

"Yes. We did." His fingers were warm and strong around hers, but she gently tugged her hand away and reached for her glass. She tried to think of a way to ask him if he was married or seeing someone, without sounding too interested.

"I have thought of you often these past few years," Miguel murmured, not seeming to notice how she was struggling with her secret. He took her left hand and brushed his thumb across her bare ring finger. "You haven't married?"

She slowly shook her head. There was only one man who'd asked her out after Tommy had been born. He was another nurse in the operating room, one of the few male nurses who worked there. She'd been tempted to date him because he was a single parent, too, and would have been a great father figure for Tommy, but in the end she hadn't been able to bring herself to accept his offer.

She hadn't felt anything for Wayne other than friendship. And as much as she wanted a father for Tommy, she couldn't pretend to feel something she didn't.

Too bad she couldn't say the same about her feelings toward Miguel. Seeing him again made her realize that she still felt that same spark of attraction, the same awareness that had been there when they'd worked together in the U.S. Feelings that apparently hadn't faded over time.

"What about you, Miguel?" she asked, taking the opening he'd offered, as she gently pulled her hand away. "Have you found a woman to marry?"

"No, you know my dream is to join Doctors Without Borders. But I can't leave until I'm certain my brother has the Vasquez olive farm back on its feet. Luis has a few—ah—problems. Things were not going well here at home during the time I was in the U.S." A shadow of guilt flashed in his eyes, and she found herself wishing she could offer him comfort.

"Not your fault, Miguel," she reminded him, secretly glad to discover he hadn't fallen in love and married a beautiful Spanish woman. "How old is Luis?"

"Twenty-six now," he said. "But too young back then to take on the responsibility of running the farm. I think the stress of trying to hold everything together was too much for my father." He stared at his glass for a long moment. "Maybe if I had been here, things would have been different."

She shrugged, not nearly as reassured as she should be at knowing his dream of joining Doctors Without Borders hadn't changed. She should be thrilled with the news. Maybe this would be best for all of them. He'd go do his mission work, leaving her alone to raise Tommy. Miguel could come back in a few years, when Tommy was older, to get to know his son.

All she had to do was to tell him the truth.

Diana wanted her to wait, but she knew she had to tell him or the secret would continue to eat at her. She'd never been any good at lying and didn't want to start now. She swallowed hard and braced herself. "Miguel, there's something important I need to tell you," she began.

"Miguel!" A shout from across the street interrupted them. She frowned and turned in time to see a handsome young man, unsteady on his feet, waving wildly at Miguel.

"Luis." He muttered his brother's name like a curse

half under his breath. "Excuse me for a moment," he said as he rose to his feet.

She didn't protest, but watched as Miguel crossed over towards his brother, his expression stern. The two of them were quickly engrossed in a heated conversation that didn't seem it would end any time soon.

Kat sat back, sipping her soft drink and thinking how wrong it was for her to be grateful for the reprieve.

"Luis, you shouldn't be drinking!" Miguel shouted in Spanish, barely holding his temper in check.

"Relax, it's Friday night. I've been slaving out at the farm all week—don't I get time to have fun too? Hey, who's the pretty Americana?" he asked with slurred speech, as he looked around Miguel towards where Katerina waited.

"She's a friend from the U.S.," he answered sharply. "But that's not the point. I thought we had an agreement? You promised to stay away from the taverns until Saturday night. It's barely five o'clock on Friday, and you're already drunk." Which meant his brother must have started drinking at least a couple of hours ago.

"I sent the last olive shipment out at noon. I think you should introduce me to your lady friend," Luis said with a sloppy smile, his gaze locked on Katerina. "She's pretty. I'd love to show her a good time."

The last thing he wanted to do was to introduce Katerina to his brother, especially when he was intoxicated. Luis had been doing fairly well recently, so finding him like this was more than a little annoying.

What was Luis thinking? If he lost the olive farm, what would he do for work? Or was this just another way to ruin Miguel's chance to follow his dream? He was tired of trying to save the olive farm for his brother while taking care of his patients. He was working non-stop from early morning to sundown every week. It was past time for Luis to grow up and take some responsibility.

"Go home, Luis," he advised. "Before you make a complete fool of yourself."

"Not until I meet your lady friend," Luis said stubbornly. "She reminds me a little of our mother, except that she has blonde hair instead of red. Are you going to change your mind about going to Africa? She may not wait for you."

Miguel ground his teeth together in frustration. "No, I'm not going to change my mind," he snapped. He didn't want to think about Katerina waiting for him. No matter how much he was still attracted to her, having a relationship with an American woman would be nothing but a disaster. His mother had hated every minute of living out on the farm, away from the city. And far away from her homeland. He was certain Katerina wouldn't be willing to leave her home either. "Katerina's sister is in the hospital, recovering from a serious head injury. She's not interested in having a good time. Leave her alone, understand?"

"Okay, fine, then." Luis shook off his hand and began walking toward the bar, his gait unsteady. "I'll just sit by myself."

"Oh, no, you won't." Miguel captured his brother's arm and caught sight of his old friend, Rafael, who happened to be a police officer. "Rafael," he called, flagging down his friend.

"Trouble, amigo?" Rafael asked, getting out of his police car.

"Would you mind taking my brother home?" He grabbed Luis's arm, steering him toward the police car, but his brother tried to resist. Luis almost fell, but Miguel managed to haul him upright. "I would take him myself, but I'm on call at the hospital."

"All right," Rafael said with a heavy sigh. "You'll owe me, my friend. Luckily for you, I'm finished with my shift."

"Thanks, Rafael. I will return the favor," he promised.

"I'll hold you to that," Rafael muttered with a wry grimace.

Miguel watched them drive away, before he raked a hand through his hair and turned back towards Katerina. As if the fates were against him, his pager went off, bringing a premature end to their time together.

"My apologies for the interruption," he murmured as he returned to the table. "I'm afraid I must cut our meal short. There is a young boy with symptoms of appendicitis. I need to return to the hospital to assess whether or not he needs surgery."

"I understand," Katerina said, as he paid the tab. She gathered up the papers he'd given to her. "Thanks again for translating Juliet's chart for me. I'm sure I'll see you tomorrow."

"Of course." When she stood, she was so close he could have easily leaned down to kiss her. He curled his fingers into fists and forced himself to take a step backwards in order to resist the sweet temptation. "I will make rounds between nine and ten in the morning, if you want an update on your sister's condition."

"Sounds good. Goodbye, Miguel." She waved and then headed for the metro station, located just a few blocks down the street.

Back at the hospital it was clear the thirteen-year-old had a classic case of appendicitis and Miguel quickly took the child to the operating room. Unfortunately, his appendix had burst, forcing Miguel to spend extra time washing out the abdominal cavity in order to minimize the chance that infection would set in. Afterwards, he made sure the boy had the correct antibiotics ordered and the first dose administered before he headed home to his three-bedroom apartment located within walking distance of the hospital.

It wasn't until he was eating cold leftover pizza for dinner that Miguel had a chance to think about Katerina, and wonder just what she'd thought was so important to tell him.

# CHAPTER THREE

"Look, it's a shopping mall!" Diana exclaimed. Then she frowned. "I almost wish my luggage hadn't shown up this morning, or I'd have a good excuse to go buy new clothes."

Kat nodded ruefully. She was surprised to find Seville was a city of contrasts, from the modern shopping mall to the mosques and bronze statues straight out of the sixteenth century. "A little disappointing in a way, isn't it?" she murmured.

"Hey, not for me," Diana pointed out. "I mean, the history here is nice and everything, but I'm all in favor of modernization. Especially when it comes to shopping."

They'd walked to a small café for breakfast, and found the shopping mall on the way back to the hotel. "Maybe you can explore the mall with Tommy this morning while I'm at the hospital, visiting Juliet."

"Sounds good. Although don't forget we plan on taking the boat tour later this afternoon," Diana reminded her.

"I won't forget," Kat murmured. Sightseeing wasn't top of her list, but it was the least she could do for Diana as her friend spent a good portion of every day watching her son. Besides, sitting for hours at the hospital wasn't going to help Juliet recover any quicker.

"Here's the metro station," Kat said. "Call me if you need anything, okay? I'll see you later, Tommy." Kat swept him into her arms for a hug, which he tolerated for barely a minute before he wiggled out of her grasp.

"We'll be fine," Diana assured her, taking Tommy's hand in a firm grip.

"I know." She watched them walk away towards the mall, before taking the steps down to the metro station to wait for the next train. Despite the fact that she still needed to break the news about Tommy to Miguel, she found she was looking forward to seeing him again. Last night, before she'd fallen asleep, Miguel's words had echoed in her mind, giving her a secret thrill.

*I've thought of you often over these past few years.*

She doubted that he'd thought of her as often as she'd thought of him, though. Mostly because of Tommy since he was the mirror image of his father. Yet also because Miguel had taken a small piece of her heart when he'd left.

Not that she ever planned on telling him that.

She needed to let go of the past and move on with her life. Whatever her conflicting feelings for Miguel, she couldn't afford to fall for him. They wanted different things out of life. She wanted a home, family, stability. Miguel wanted adventure. He wanted Doctors Without Borders. He wanted to travel. The only time they were in sync was when they had worked as colleagues in the O.R..

And, of course, during the night they spent together.

Walking into the hospital was familiar now, and she

greeted the clerk behind the desk in Spanish. *"Buenos dias."*

*"Buenos dias,"* the clerk replied with a wide grin. One thing about Spain, most people seemed to be in a good mood. Maybe because they had a more laid-back lifestyle here. She found it amazing that the shops actually closed down for three hours between noon and three for siesta. She couldn't imagine anyone in the U.S. doing something like that.

Yet if the people were happier, maybe it was worth it?

Kat took the stairs to the third-floor I.C.U., entered her sister's room and crossed over to the bedside, taking her sister's small hand in hers. "Hi, Jules, I'm back. How are you feeling, hmm?"

She knew her sister wasn't going to open her eyes and start talking, which would be impossible with a breathing tube in anyway, but Kat was convinced patients even in her sister's condition could hear what was going on around them, so she decided she'd keep up her one-sided conversation with her sister.

"Seville is a beautiful city, Jules, I can understand why you wanted to study here. I wish I knew exactly what happened to you. No one here seems to know anything more than the fact that you ran into the road and were struck by a car. Can you hear me, Jules? If you can hear me, squeeze my hand."

When Juliet's fingers squeezed hers, Kat's knees nearly buckled in relief. "That's great, Juliet. Now wiggle your toes for me. Can you wiggle your toes?"

This time Juliet's non-casted left leg moved again. It wasn't wiggling her toes, exactly, but Kat was still thrilled at the small movement. Her sister was truly doing better. Juliet would probably only follow commands intermittently, but each day she'd improve and do better.

Exactly the way Miguel had assured her she would.

"Good job, Jules. I'm so glad you can hear me. You're still in the hospital in Seville, but as soon as you're better, you're going to be sent to an American hospital back home. Can you understand what I'm saying? If you can understand me, squeeze my hand."

Juliet squeezed her hand again, and relieved tears blurred her vision. Her sister was going to make it. Juliet might have a long road to recovery ahead of her, but she was going to make it.

"Katerina?"

At the sound of Miguel's voice she whirled around and quickly crossed over to him. "She's following commands, Miguel!" she exclaimed. "She's starting to wake up!"

He caught her close in a warm hug. "I'm glad," he murmured, his mouth dangerously close to her ear.

She wanted to wrap her arms around his waist and lean on his strength, but she forced herself to step away, putting badly needed distance between them. What was wrong with her? It wasn't as if she'd come to Seville in order to rejuvenate her feelings for Miguel. Better for her if she kept him firmly in the friendship category. As if their one night together had been an aberration.

One that had produced a son.

There was no reason to feel as if being around Miguel was like coming home. Truthfully, she'd never been farther from home.

"I'm sorry," she said, wiping her tears on the back

of her hand while searching for a tissue. "I didn't mean to get all emotional on you."

"Here." He grabbed the box of tissues from the bedside table and handed them to her. "Don't apologize, I know how worried you've been."

She blew her nose and pulled herself together, forcing a smile. "I hope this doesn't mean you're going to send Juliet home right away, are you?"

"Not yet. I would like your sister to be completely off the ventilator and more awake before she's transported back to the U.S."

"Sounds good." She was relieved to know they wouldn't have to leave Seville just yet. Especially as she hadn't told Miguel about Tommy. A wave of guilt hit hard. Should she tell him now? No, this wasn't exactly the time or the place for a heavy conversation. Besides, Miguel was working, making rounds. No doubt he had many patients to see.

She was about to ask him what time he got off work when he reached over to take her hand in his. "Katerina, will you have dinner with me tonight?"

She hesitated just a moment before nodding her assent. Wasn't this what she'd wanted all along? A good time and place to tell him about his son? A quiet dinner with just the two of them would be the perfect time to give him the news. "Yes, Miguel. Dinner would be wonderful."

"Excellent," he murmured. His gaze was warm and she had to remind herself this wasn't a date. Her son's future was what mattered here, not her roller-coaster feelings for his father.

"What time?" she asked.

"We'll go early as I know you're not used to our customs yet. Shall we say eight o'clock?"

A wry grin tugged at the corner of her mouth because eight o'clock wasn't at all early back home. "All right. Where should I meet you?"

"I will pick you up at your hotel. Which one are you staying at?"

"We— I'm at the Hesperia hotel," she said, using the correct Spanish pronunciation while hoping he didn't catch her slip.

"Excellent. There is a wonderful restaurant just a few blocks away." He glanced at his watch. "I'm sorry, but I need to finish making rounds. Did you have any questions about the chart copies I gave you?"

She'd read through his entire stack of notes early that morning, before Tommy had woken up. "I noticed her electrolytes keep going out of whack—do you think that's because of her head injury?"

"Yes, brain injuries cause sodium levels to drop, but try not to worry as we are replacing what she's lost."

She'd noticed the IV solution running through Juliet's IV was similar to what they'd use in the U.S. Except for the equipment being a little different, the basics of medical and nursing care were very much the same.

"Thanks again, Miguel, for everything," she said in a low voice, trying to put the depth of her feelings into words. "I'm so relieved to know my sister is in such good hands."

"You're very welcome, Katerina. I'll see you tonight, yes?"

"Yes," she confirmed. After he left, she walked back and sat down at her sister's bedside.

She was lucky that Miguel was here. Not just because he spoke English, which was a huge help, but because she knew he was an excellent surgeon.

Ironic how fate had brought her face to face with Tommy's father after all these years. Her previously suppressed feelings for Miguel threatened to surface and she took a long, deep breath, ruthlessly shoving them back down.

She needed to protect her heart from Miguel's charm. And even more importantly, she needed to preserve the life she'd built with her son.

Miguel finished his rounds and then took a break to call his brother. Unfortunately, Luis didn't answer the phone so he left his brother a message, requesting a return phone call.

He rubbed the back of his neck, debating whether he should go out to see his brother after work or not. He should have time before dinner as he wasn't on call this evening. But at the same time, going all the way out to the farm and back would take at least two and a half hours, and he didn't want to be late for his dinner date with Katerina.

Miguel was pleased Katerina had agreed to see him again tonight. He felt the need to make it up to her for leaving so abruptly after finding out about his father's stroke. The night they'd spent together had been incredible. There had always been the hint of awareness between them while working together in the operating room. At times it had seemed as if Katerina could practically read his mind, instinctively knowing what he'd needed before he'd had to ask.

He'd been tempted to pursue a relationship, but had told himself it wouldn't be fair since he wasn't planning on staying. Maybe if things had been different...

No, he'd made his decision. He'd already given notice at the hospital that he was leaving at the end of the academic year, which was just three months away. He'd first heard about Doctors Without Borders in Madrid from one of his colleagues. He'd quickly decided that he wanted to join as well once he'd finished his training. He'd known early on he didn't want to stay on his family's olive farm. He'd wanted to travel. To learn about other cultures. He'd jumped at the opportunity to study in the U.S. and now couldn't wait to join Doctors Without Borders.

So why was he torturing himself by seeing Katerina again? If he had a functioning brain cell in his head, he'd stay far away from her until her sister was stable enough for transport back home.

Katerina wasn't the woman for him. He knew he shouldn't measure all women against his American mother, but after living in both cultures he understood a little better why his mother had reacted the way she had. The two lifestyles were very different. Maybe if the olive farm hadn't suffered two bad years in a row, there would have been money for vacations back in the U.S. Would that have been enough for his mother? Or would that have only emphasized her loss?

Truthfully, he couldn't understand why his mother just hadn't purchased a one-way ticket to New York and returned home if she'd been so desperately unhappy here. Instead, she'd stayed to become a bitter woman who'd made all their lives miserable. Until she'd unexpectedly died of an overdose, which had been determined to be accidental rather than a suicide attempt.

Miguel shook off his dark thoughts and concentrated on his patients. He loved everything about being a surgeon. There wasn't nearly as much trauma here in Seville as in Cambridge, Massachusetts, but he didn't mind. One thing he never got used to was losing patients.

Especially young patients. Like the twenty-five-year-old pregnant mother they'd lost during his last shift in the U.S.

After finishing his rounds on the adults in his case load, he made his way over to the children's wing, which happened to be in the oldest part of the hospital. He wanted to visit Pedro, his young appendectomy patient. The young boy would need to stay a few days for IV antibiotics before he could be discharged.

This was the other part he loved about being a doctor in Spain. There weren't large children's hospitals here, the way there were in the U.S. He was glad to have the opportunity to take care of both children and adults, rather than being forced to decide between them.

"*Hola,* Dr. Vasquez," Pedro greeted him when he entered the room.

"*Hola, Pedro. ¿Como estas?*"

"*¿*English, *por favor*? I'm fine."

Miguel grinned and switched to English for Pedro's sake. The youngster was part of a group of teenagers in Seville who were committed to learning English. Many of them didn't bother, but even when Pedro had been in pain in the emergency department yesterday, the boy had informed him he was going to America one day.

"May I examine your incision?" Miguel asked politely.

Pedro frowned, probably having trouble with the word "incision", but lifted his hospital gown anyway. "It's healing well, no?"

"Very much so," Miguel said, pleased to see there were no signs of infection. Although the bigger problem Pedro faced was an infection in the bloodstream from the burst appendix. "Where is your mother? I think you'll need to stay for a couple more days yet."

Pedro smiled broadly as he drew his hospital gown back down. "She's caring for my younger brothers and sisters. She'll be here soon. And I'm glad to stay, Dr. Vasquez, because you will have more time for me to practice my English with you, yes?"

Miguel couldn't help but grin at the awkwardly worded sentence. "Yes, Pedro. We will practice while you are here, but even after you go home, we can practice when you return to clinic to see me, okay?"

"Okay. Thanks, Dr. Vasquez."

Miguel went on to see his second patient, a young girl who'd sustained a compound fracture of her left arm. They had orthopedic specialists, but since the fracture wasn't complicated he'd simply set it himself and casted it.

Marissa's room was empty so Miguel went to find the nurse, only to discover that the young girl was getting another X-ray of her arm.

He decided to return to the I.C.U., vowing to come back to check on Marissa later, but as he reached the third floor, the entire building shook and the lights flickered and went out. It took him a moment to realize what had happened, even though he'd been through this scenario once before.

Earthquake!


Kat was about to leave the I.C.U., intending to head back to the hotel, when she felt the building shake with enough force to make her fall against the wall.

The lights flickered and then went out. She froze, waiting for them to come back on.

Juliet's ventilator!

Instinctively, she ran back down the hall to her sister's room, able to see somewhat from the daylight shining through the windows. She saw Miguel going into another room but didn't veer from her path. After rushing over to Juliet's bedside, she reached for the ambu-bag hanging from the oxygen regulator. She turned the dial up, providing high-flow oxygen as she quickly disconnected the ventilator and began assisting her sister's breathing.

She forced herself to calm down so she wouldn't hyperventilate Juliet, hardly able to believe that the power was still out. Didn't they have back-up generators here? What had caused the shaking? Did they have earthquakes here? And where was everyone? She'd hadn't seen anyone other than the glimpse of Miguel going into another patient's room.

After what seemed like forever, the lights flickered back on, but only part way, as if conserving energy. At least Juliet's ventilator and heart monitor came back on.

She connected the ventilator back up to Juliet's breathing tube, but before she could go out and find the rest of the hospital staff, Miguel showed up in the doorway.

"What happened?" she asked.

"Earthquake. Nothing too serious, probably about a five or six on the Richter scale. We've had one similar to this before. But I need your help."

Earthquake? She was a little shocked, but strove to remain calm. "Me? What for?"

"I've just been told that a very old tree fell against the corner of the building and we need to evacuate the patients. They are all pediatric patients in the children's wing located on the fourth floor. As it is a weekend, we do not have full staffing. We could use an extra pair of hands if you're willing to stay?"

"Of course," she said, knowing she couldn't simply walk away, even though she needed to know her son was safe. She was tempted to call Diana right away, except that she didn't want Miguel to ask questions. So she promised herself she'd wait until she could steal a few minutes alone to call her friend.

"Let's go," Miguel said, and she followed him out of the I.C.U. and down the hall, trying to make sense of what was happening. Clearly, the earthquake must have caused the tree to fall on the hospital building. What other damage had occurred? And what about the hotel? Was everything all right there?

As they walked down the hall, she peered through the windows to look out over the city. She was relieved when she didn't see any evidence of mass destruction. As she followed Miguel, she hoped and prayed Tommy and Diana were someplace safe from harm.

# CHAPTER FOUR

KAT was horrified to see the amount of damage the building had sustained when they arrived in the children's ward. Many of the younger kids were crying, but one older boy had already stepped up to take charge. He'd obviously gathered all the children on several beds located as far away as possible from the crumbled corner of the building.

"Good job, Pedro," Miguel said as they rushed in. "Where's your nurse, Elouisa?"

"I'm not sure, but I think she went to get medication," Pedro answered. Kat was impressed that the boy spoke English and seemed to accept the responsibility of staying here with the children alone.

Miguel's mouth tightened, but he didn't say anything else. "Okay, then, we'll need to transport the sickest patients down to the I.C.U. first."

"DiCarlo is the worst, I think," Pedro said, pointing to a boy who was lying listlessly in bed. Kat estimated there were at least a dozen kids gathered on three beds surrounding the obviously very sick boy. "Elouisa said something about how he needed more antibiotics."

"She should have stayed here with all of you. He can get his antibiotics in the I.C.U.," Miguel said firmly.

"I'll take him down, but do you think it's safe to use the elevators?" she asked warily. She didn't mind transporting the sick child downstairs but the thought of being stuck in an elevator alone with him was scary.

Just then Elouisa returned, hurrying in with an IV bag in her hand. She came straight over to DiCarlo's IV pump to prepare the medication.

Miguel said something to her in Spanish, which she assumed was something related to the care of the children. She responded in Spanish as well, even while she hung the IV antibiotic. When they finished their conversation, Miguel turned to her.

"Okay, you and I together will take DiCarlo in his bed down to the I.C.U. Elouisa has promised to stay with the children." He turned to Pedro. "I am counting on you to stay here and to help Elouisa until I can return, okay? Once we have DiCarlo safe in the I.C.U., we can find other beds for the rest of you."

Pedro nodded. "I understand Dr. Vasquez. You should have trust that I will wait here for you."

"Good, Pedro. Thank you."

"Give me a quick rundown on DiCarlo's condition," she said to Miguel as Elouisa used an old-fashioned crank to lift the bed higher off the floor so it would be easier for them to push him. "I need to understand what to watch for."

Miguel set a small bin of emergency supplies on DiCarlo's bed, and again she was struck by the similarities between medical care here in Seville and in the U.S. When she worked in the I.C.U., they would always take a small pack of emergency supplies on what they called road trips, when patients needed to leave the I.C.U. to go down for certain X-rays or CT scans. Miguel started pushing the boy's bed towards the elevator as he gave a brief report.

"What started as pneumonia has turned into full-blown sepsis. He's been fighting the infection as best he can, but he's had heart trouble since he was born so he's not as strong as most children his age."

She digested that bit of information as they left the children's ward through a long, empty hallway. As they waited for the elevator, which seemed to take a very long time, she looked down at DiCarlo's wan features, hoping and praying he'd survive the infection.

Miguel's impatience was obvious when he stabbed the elevator button a second time.

"Where is everyone?" she asked. Miguel's features tightened. "We were short-staffed to begin with, but some left, wanting to check on their loved ones. I honestly didn't think we would lose this many staff members."

She could understand why some staff had felt compelled to leave, and worry over the safety of her son gnawed at her. She pushed her fears aside. For one thing, Diana would have called her if something bad had happened. Their hotel was new and sturdy. Surely they'd be safe. The elevator arrived and she helped Miguel push DiCarlo's bed inside. The doors closed and she pushed the button for the second floor when suddenly the boy began coughing so hard his face turned bright red.

"Miguel, he's having trouble breathing," she said urgently, reaching for the dial on the oxygen tank and turning the knob to give him more oxygen. "Do we have a pediatric ambu bag?"

"Yes, along with intubation supplies." Miguel opened the small bag of emergency supplies and pulled out the ambu bag. "We can intubate if we have to."

She hadn't assisted with an intubation since the time she'd worked in the I.C.U., but she nodded anyway. She gently placed the small face mask over DiCarlo's mouth and nose, and used the ambu bag to give him a couple of breaths.

DiCarlo squirmed beneath the ambu bag, fighting her at first, but then abruptly went limp, and she quickly reached over to feel for a pulse. "Miguel? His pulse is fading fast."

"I'll have to intubate him now, rather than waiting until we reach the I.C.U." He took the laryngoscope in his left hand and then gently slid the endotracheal tube into DiCarlo's throat. She took Miguel's stethoscope from around his neck and listened to the boy's lungs to verify the tube was in the correct place. Thankfully, it was. She quickly connected the ambu bag tubing to the end of the endotracheal tube so she could give DiCarlo several breaths.

Miguel secured the tube with tape and then gestured behind her. "Check his pulse and then push the button again. The doors have already closed."

She'd never heard the elevator ding. She made sure DiCarlo's pulse was stable before she turned around to hit the button for the third floor. This time it only took a couple of minutes for the doors to open.

She was very happy to see the critical care area. "Which bed?" she asked, as she walked backwards, pulling the bed as Miguel pushed, keeping one hand on the child's endotracheal tube.

"Twelve," he directed.

She knew the basic layout of the unit from visiting her sister and quickly pulled the bed towards the vacant room number twelve. Nurses came over and assisted her with getting DiCarlo connected to the heart monitor overheard.

*"Gracias,"* she murmured, smiling weakly. She glanced up and was reassured to note that DiCarlo's pulse had stabilized. Miguel spoke to them in Spanish, and they quickly brought over a ventilator. She stepped back, allowing the staff room to work.

Crisis averted, at least for the moment.

She hesitated, not sure if she should go back down to the children's wing alone or wait for Miguel. He was still examining DiCarlo, and the grave concern in his gaze as he listened to the boy's lungs wrenched her heart.

Would he look at Tommy like that?

Just then he glanced up and caught her staring at him. She swallowed the lump in her throat, holding his gaze for a long moment. Watching him, the way he was so gentle with DiCarlo, gave her hope and reassurance that he would never do anything to hurt their son. Including taking him away from her.

"He's fine for now," Miguel said, putting his stethoscope away. "Give me a few minutes here while I make sure his orders are up to date."

"Of course," she murmured, turning away, her hand on her phone. Outside DiCarlo's room, she made sure she was out of Miguel's hearing distance before she quickly pressed the number for Diana, holding her breath while she waited for an answer. Diana's voice brought instant relief. "Kat? Are you okay?"

"Yes. Are you and Tommy safe? Was there damage to the hotel?"

"We lost power for a while, and there seems to be a lot of confusion, but we're fine. No damage to the hotel that we know of."

Kat closed her eyes with relief. "I'm so glad. Listen, I have to stay here for a bit yet—will you be okay for a while?"

"Sure. We'll be fine."

"Thanks, I'll check in with you later." She closed her phone just as Miguel came around the corner of the nurses' station. She quickly tucked the phone back into her pocket.

"Ready to go?" Miguel asked.

"Of course." She felt bad for deceiving him, but obviously this wasn't the time or place for a conversation about his son. As they walked together toward the stairwell, their hands brushed lightly. A tingle of awareness shot up her arm.

"So, maybe I should apply to be a nurse here, huh?" she said jokingly, in a feeble attempt to break the closeness that seemed to grow deeper between them every moment they spent together.

"Are you planning to stay?" he asked, in shocked surprise. The brief flash of horror in his eyes pierced the tiny balloon of hope that had begun to grow in her heart.

"No! Of course not. That was a joke, Miguel." Ridiculous to be hurt that he didn't want her to stay. She preceded him down the stairwell, wondering if he'd change his opinion once she told him about Tommy.

She had to tell him about his son. The sooner, the better.

\* \* \*

Miguel mentally smacked himself on the side of the head, understanding from the stiffness in her shoulders and the sharpness of her tone that he'd inadvertently hurt her.

He hadn't meant to make it sound like he didn't want her to stay. He'd just been taken aback by her statement, especially after they'd worked together to save DiCarlo. He couldn't help making comparisons with his mother. Maybe if his mother had been able to work in a career, other than helping his father run the olive farm, she would have been happier.

Could Katerina really be happy in Seville? And why did it matter as he himself wasn't planning to stay?

He hadn't slept well last night because all he'd been able to think about had been Katerina. And even now, in the aftermath of a small earthquake, he still wanted her.

But their situation was no different than it had been back when he'd met her in Cambridge. He'd already committed to Doctors Without Borders. He was finally going to live his dream. He couldn't start something with Katerina that he wasn't willing to finish.

A tiny voice in the back of his mind wondered if she'd be willing to go with him. But then he remembered Juliet. No, the Katerina he knew wouldn't pack up and leave her sister. Especially not when Juliet had a potentially long road of recovery ahead of her. Several months of rehab at least.

He pushed thoughts of Katerina possibly going with him to Africa aside to concentrate on the situation down in the children's ward.

Thankfully, Elouisa had kept her word, staying with

the rest of the children. He was glad to see an additional staff nurse had come up to help.

"Which wing can we use as the children's ward?" he asked, joining the group. "I'd like to keep them together if possible."

"We can use the east wing of the third floor," Elouisa informed him. "I too would like to keep them together if possible. How is DiCarlo?"

"Very ill. We had to intubate him in the elevator," Miguel said. "You were right to make sure he received his antibiotic," he said by way of apology. He'd been upset to find the children alone, but he understood she'd prioritized the best she could.

"I was hoping to get him to the I.C.U.," Elouisa admitted. "But you were right, I shouldn't have left the children alone."

"Difficult decision either way, so don't worry about it." He noticed Pedro was listening to their conversation. He was impressed with how the boy had taken charge in Elouisa's absence. "Pedro, are you able to walk or would you like us to get you a wheelchair?"

Pedro practically puffed out his chest. "I can walk. I'm fine, Dr. Vasquez."

He could tell Pedro had some pain, but the boy wasn't about to admit it. He vowed to make sure Pedro took some pain medication as soon as they were all relocated in their new rooms.

Elouisa gathered up several wheelchairs and between the three of them they assisted getting all the children ready for transport. Pedro helped, as if he were a hospital staff member rather than one of the patients needing to be relocated.

The elevator was too small for everyone to go at once, so Elouisa and Pedro took three children first, while the second nurse, Maria, took two patients with her. Miguel and Katerina waited for the next elevator with their three patients. They were lucky there hadn't been more patients in the children's wing.

"Pedro's English is amazing," Katerina said while they waited for the elevator. "I'm impressed at how he seems to understand everything we're saying."

"He takes learning English very seriously as he is determined to go to America one day," he admitted. "You'd never know he had a burst appendix last evening, would you?"

Katerina's eyes widened. "No, I certainly wouldn't. He's doing remarkably well."

"Yes, but as his appendix ruptured, I want him to get a good twenty-four to forty-eight hours of IV antibiotics before he's discharged."

The elevator arrived and as they quickly maneuvered the three remaining patients into the elevator, Miguel found himself watching Katerina with awe. He'd always known she was an excellent O.R. nurse but seeing her interact with the young patients, managing to overcome the language barrier with smiles, simple words and hand gestures, he thought her skills would be better utilized in a position where she could care for awake and alert patients on the ward or in the I.C.U.

Or in the Doctors Without Borders program. They needed nurses to work with them, too.

Not that her career choices were any of his business.

It didn't take long to get the children settled on the east wing of the third floor. The entire layout of the area was very similar to the one where the building had collapsed. Even Pedro reluctantly took to his bed, and Miguel made sure he took a dose of pain medication that was long overdue.

Afterwards, he glanced at his watch, thinking he should go up and check on DiCarlo. But he was hesitant to leave Elouisa here alone as Maria had been called away to help elsewhere. He walked up to the nurses' desk where Elouisa was busy organizing the charts. "Have you requested additional nursing support?" he asked.

"*Sí,* but so far Maria has not returned," she told him. "Thankfully, most of the children are very stable, especially now that DiCarlo is in the I.C.U."

"True, but I still think you should have someone with you. What if you have to leave the unit for some reason?"

Katerina stepped forward. "I can stay for a while," she volunteered. "I would just like a few minutes to check on my sister first."

He nodded, filled with gratitude. Even though Katerina wasn't licensed to practice nursing here in Seville, she could stay on the unit as a volunteer, offering a second pair of hands as needed. And her knowledge of nursing would be invaluable. He would feel much better knowing Elouisa wasn't here on the children's wing alone.

"Why don't you run over to see your sister, and I will wait here until you return?" he offered.

"*Gracias,*" she murmured. "I promise to be quick."

He couldn't begrudge her the chance to make sure Juliet's condition hadn't changed since they'd been up there. "I will need to check on her too, but I will wait for you to return."

"*¿Que?*" Elouisa asked, indicating she hadn't understood his conversation, so he quickly translated for her. "Both of you go and check on her sister," Elouisa said firmly. "I will be fine alone here for five minutes until Katerina returns. Pedro has been a huge help. He will get help in an emergency."

Miguel reluctantly agreed and led the way down to the I.C.U., using the stairwell as the elevator was so slow.

"You're going to have to make Pedro an honorary nurse, soon," Katerina teased as they walked towards Juliet's room. "Maybe after all this he'll decide to pursue a career in medicine?"

He chuckled. "There are not nearly as many male nurses here in Seville as there are back in America."

They entered Juliet's room and Katerina immediately crossed over to take her sister's hand. "I'm here, Jules," she said in a gentle tone. "Don't worry, you're still doing fine."

Juliet was moving restlessly on the bed, as if she was uncomfortable. Katerina tried to comfort her, talking to her in a soothing voice as Miguel took the clipboard off the foot of the bed and scanned the latest laboratory results and vital signs that had been recorded.

"Miguel?" He glanced up at Katerina's urgent tone. "Look! I think she's having a seizure!"

# CHAPTER FIVE

"Disconnect the ventilator and use the ambu bag to assist her breathing," he directed quickly. He leaned over to hit the emergency call light and in less than thirty seconds two nurses came running in. He gave them orders in Spanish for a loading dose of IV dilantin followed by a continuous infusion. Also five milligrams of Versed to calm the effects of the seizure and for new IV fluids to correct Juliet's electrolyte imbalance.

His heart twisted when he saw the sheen of tears in Katerina's eyes. Thankfully, the seizure didn't last long, and within ten minutes he was able to put Juliet back on the ventilator. The medications he'd ordered worked beautifully, and Kat looked relieved when Juliet was resting quietly in her bed.

"She's going to be okay," he murmured to Katerina as they moved back, allowing the nurses to complete the dilantin infusion along with the new IV fluids he'd ordered. "This isn't a sign that her head injury is worse, but more likely as a result of her electrolyte imbalance."

Katerina rubbed her hands over her arms, as if she was cold, and he couldn't stop himself from putting a strong arm around her shoulders and drawing her close. "Are you going to do a CT scan of her head, just to be sure this isn't related to her intracranial hemorrhage?" she asked.

He hesitated because normally he wouldn't order such a test for that purpose. But he found himself wanting to reassure her in any way possible. "Let's wait to see how she does after the electrolytes are in, okay? If there is any change in her neuro status, I will order the scan immediately."

Katerina pulled away from him, turning to look at her sister, and he sensed she wasn't happy with his decision.

He wasn't used to explaining himself—especially not to a family member of a patient. "Listen to me, the earthquake has caused some chaos here in the hospital. I see now that your sister didn't get the new IV fluids I'd ordered during rounds. I truly believe, Katerina, her seizure is the result of an electrolyte imbalance."

She swiped a hand over her eyes, sniffed loudly and nodded. "All right, Miguel, we can wait to see how she does once the electrolytes are corrected."

He reached out to put a hand on her shoulder, wanting nothing more than to offer comfort, easing her fears. "I promise you, I'll take good care of your sister, Katerina."

For a moment he didn't think she'd respond, but then she suddenly turned and threw herself into his arms. Surprised and pleased, he hugged her close.

"I can't lose her, Miguel. I just can't," she said in a muffled voice. "I promised my mother I'd take care of her. She has to be okay, she just has to!"

Her despair tore at his heart. "I know, Katerina," he whispered, brushing his cheek against her silky hair, ignoring the shocked stares from the two nurses. "I know."

As soon as the IV medications were flowing according to his prescribed rate, the two nurses left them alone in the room. He continued to hold Katerina close, smoothing a hand down her back, giving her the emotional support she needed while trying to ignore the sexual awareness zinging through his bloodstream. He was stunned to realize how much he wanted her, even after all this time. And the feeling was impossibly stronger than it had been during the night they'd shared together four and a half years ago.

He hadn't left her by choice, returning home because of his father's stroke, but he hadn't sought her out afterwards, either. Had he made a mistake? Was he wrong not to have gone back to be with her again?

He pressed a kiss along her temple and the slight caress must have been too much for her because she pulled away abruptly, straightening her spine and swiping at the wetness on her face. "I'm sorry, Miguel. I don't know what's wrong with me. I'm usually not this much of a mess."

"Give yourself a break, Katerina. It's understandable that you're worried about your sister. And this has been incredibly stressful for all of us. Despite what you may think, we don't have earthquakes here often." He lifted a hand to wipe a strand of hair from her cheek. "You don't have to stay to help if you don't want to. Maybe you should go back to the hotel for some rest."

She bit her lower lip and he could sense her inner struggle, knowing she was tempted to take him up on his offer. But then she sighed and shook her head. "I can't leave Elouisa all alone with those sick children. I will stay, but only for an hour or so. Hopefully by then, some of the staff will have returned."

He nodded, admiring her strength and determination. "I would like to think so, too."

For a moment she simply stared at him, and then she totally shocked him by putting her hand on his chest and going up on tiptoe to kiss his cheek. It was everything he could do not to pull her into his arms for a real kiss. The feather-light touch was too brief and before he could blink, she drew away. "I'll see you later, Miguel," she whispered, before leaving to return to the children's ward.

His throat was so tight, he couldn't speak. He spent several long minutes wrestling his warring emotions under control. Part of him knew he was playing with fire, yet he couldn't stay away from Katerina. Couldn't keep himself at arm's distance. He longed to kiss her. To make love to her.

Taking a deep breath, he tried to relax his tense muscles. He hadn't forgotten their dinner plans for later this evening, but with the earthquake there was a possibility the restaurants would be closed.

But he refused to consider breaking their date. No, he could always cook for her at his place, if necessary.

The idea grew on him as he continued to make rounds on his patients. He would be happy to prepare Katerina a meal she would never forget. And maybe they could explore the attraction that simmered between them.

Kat tried to concentrate on distracting the children, but she couldn't stop worrying about her sister and her son.

Even though she'd spoken to Diana just a little over an hour ago, she wanted to talk to her again.

Tommy was pretty young to talk on the phone, but she needed to hear his voice, just for a moment.

She ducked into a bathroom, seeking a moment of privacy. She called Diana again, and her friend answered right away. "Hi, Kat."

"Diana, I'm sorry, but I'm still here at the hospital. Some of the staff left and I'm volunteering on the children's ward. How's Tommy?"

"He misses you, but we've been playing video games since the power has come back on. Truly, he's fine."

"Can I talk to him? Just for a minute?"

"Sure, just a sec. Tommy, say hi to your mama, okay? Say hi," she urged.

"Hi, Mama." Tears pricked her eyelids when she heard her son's voice.

"Hi, Tommy. I love you very much. Be good for Aunt Diana, okay?"

There was a moment of silence and then Diana came back on the line. "I know you can't see him, but he's nodding in agreement to whatever you said, Kat."

Knowing that made her smile. "I'm glad. I told him to be good for you. Diana, I'm sorry we can't go on the boat ride," she murmured. "Maybe things will be back to normal tomorrow."

"Sure. Just come back as soon as you can, okay?"

"I will. Take good care of Tommy for me." Kat had to force herself to hang up, or she'd be bawling again.

Okay, she needed to get a grip here. She was becoming an emotional basket case. She quickly used the facilities and then splashed cold water on her face, pulling herself together.

As she returned to the children's ward, she found herself looking for Miguel. Ridiculous, as he was obviously spending time with the sicker patients. She hoped DiCarlo was doing better as she made rounds on the sick children, pleased to note they were doing fairly well.

She saved Pedro for last, knowing he'd want time to talk. "How are you, Pedro?"

"Very good, miss," he said, although his smile was strained, betraying his pain.

"Please, call me Kat," she instructed, coming over to stand beside his bed. "When was the last time you took a dose of pain medication?"

He shrugged one thin shoulder and angled his chin. "I'm fine. I'm not sick like these other children."

"Pedro, you had surgery less than twenty-four hours ago," she reminded him gently. "Taking pain medicine is not a sign of weakness. You need to conserve your strength so your body can heal."

She watched as he seemed to consider her words. "Maybe it is time for a pill," he agreed reluctantly.

"I will ask Elouisa to come," she said, turning toward the door.

"Miss Kat?" His voice stopped her.

"Yes, Pedro, what is it?"

"Are you and Dr. Vasquez..." He paused and frowned, as if searching for the right word. "Boyfriend and girlfriend?" he asked finally.

She couldn't hide her shock. "No! Why would you ask something like that, Pedro?"

His dark eyes crinkled with humor. "Because to me

it seems that you like each other very much," he said reasonably.

"Of course we like each other, we're friends, Pedro. We're friends, nothing more," she said firmly, trying not to blush. The boy was too observant by far. She really needed to keep her emotions under strict control. "I will go and get your pain medicine, which you will take, okay?"

She didn't wait for his response, but went out to find Elouisa. So far, she and the nurse had managed to communicate with facial expressions and hand gestures, intermixed with brief phrases.

"Pedro—medication *para dolor*," she said, using the Spanish word for pain. She found it amazing how the occasional word from her two years of high-school Spanish flashed in her memory.

"*Sí,* okay." Elouisa seemed to know right away what she meant. As the nurse went to get the pain medication, she couldn't help glancing at her watch. She'd been here almost an hour, and as much as she wanted to stay and help, she also longed to return to the hotel to see her son.

Surprisingly, it was only two o'clock in the afternoon, although it seemed as if she'd been here at the hospital for ever. She vowed to stay just another thirty minutes and no longer. For one thing, she was very hungry. And for another, she wanted to hold her son close, kiss his cheek and reassure herself that he was truly okay.

Elouisa returned, holding out a small paper medication cup, very similar to the ones they used in the hospital back home. Kat and Elouisa went back to Pedro's room to give him his medicine.

They found him standing in the doorway, a frightened expression on his face. "Pedro? What's wrong?"

He brought his hand away from his abdomen, revealing a bright crimson stain spreading across his hospital gown. "I'm bleeding," he said, as if he could hardly believe it.

"Elouisa, call Dr. Vasquez, Hurry! *¡Rapidamente!*" The nurse rushed for the phone while she quickly crossed over to put her arm around Pedro's shoulders. "You've broken open your stitches," she told him calmly. "Come, now, you need to get back to bed."

Pedro murmured something in Spanish, and the fact that he was too stunned to practice his English worried her more than the blood staining his gown. She should have inspected his incision. "Stay still, Pedro, Dr. Vasquez will be here soon."

True to her word, Miguel strode in just moments later. "What happened?"

"I'm not sure," she was forced to admit. "I knew he was having pain, but I didn't realize he'd broken open his stitches."

"Everything he did today was too much for him." Miguel's compassionate gaze did not hold any blame.

"I should have examined his incision," she admitted softly. "I'm sorry, Miguel."

He shook his head as he turned toward Pedro. "Do not take this on yourself, Katerina. Will you please get me some gauze dressings? I need to see how bad the wound looks."

She knew he was trying to offer Pedro some privacy and quickly left the room, searching for the supply cart. She found the gauze without too much trouble and then returned to Pedro's room, hovering outside the doorway until she knew the boy was adequately covered.

"Do you have the gauze?" Miguel called, indicating it was safe to enter.

"Yes." The sheets were arranged so that his body was covered except for his belly. The small gaping hole in Pedro's abdomen worried her, although she tried not to let it show. "Will he need to go back to surgery?" she asked as she opened the gauze packet for him, keeping the contents sterile.

He took the gauze with his gloved fingers and turned back to Pedro. "I'm afraid so. Pedro, I will need to fix this open incision right away, understand?" He spoke in Spanish too, likely repeating what he'd said.

"I understand," Pedro murmured.

"You'll need to talk to his mother. I'll ask Elouisa to get hold of her."

"Thanks."

She left the room, and made sure Elouisa understood she needed to call Pedro's *madre* before she returned. Miguel had just finished dressing the wound, stepping back and stripping off his soiled gloves. "I will call down to surgery to make sure they have a room available and staff to assist."

She chewed her lower lip nervously. "And what if they don't have staff to assist?" she asked.

Miguel hesitated. "I'm afraid I will have to ask for your assistance, Katerina. You are a skilled O.R. nurse and we have worked together many times."

She opened her mouth to protest but stopped herself, realizing Pedro was listening to the interaction between them. She didn't want to say anything to upset the boy. "I can certainly help as needed," she agreed.

Miguel hurried away, apparently to make the necessary phone calls. She forced a reassuring smile on her face as she crossed over to Pedro's bedside, taking his hand in hers. "You're going to be fine, Pedro. Dr. Vasquez is a very talented surgeon. He will fix you up in no time."

"Will you assist him, Miss Kat?" Pedro asked, his eyes betraying a flicker of fear. "If there is no one else?"

"Of course I will do whatever is needed, Pedro. Don't you worry about a thing, okay? You're going to be fine."

*"Gracias,"* he murmured, tightening his grip on her hand.

When Miguel returned, the tense expression on his face told her without words that her help would be needed. "There is a theater available, but the staff nurses who have stayed and the surgeon on call are busy with a trauma patient. Either Pedro waits until they are finished or you come down to assist me. It's your choice, Katerina. I know I have asked a lot from you today."

She didn't hesitate, knowing she could never let Pedro down. "I will be happy to help," she said firmly.

Miguel flashed a grateful smile. "Thank you, Katerina. This is a small surgery and shouldn't take too long."

She glanced down at Pedro's small brown hand clasped tightly in hers. She couldn't have left him any more than she could have left her own son. "I know. Remember, Pedro, Dr. Vasquez and I have worked together often in America. We made a good team."

"Yes, we did." Miguel's soft tone reminded her of

the night he'd made love to her. She needed to protect her heart from his lethal charm.

"Dr. Vasquez?" Elouisa poked her head into the room and said something about Pedro's mother. Miguel excused himself and went out to take the call.

Within minutes he'd returned. "Your mother will try to be here soon, but I'd rather not wait if that's okay. I need to repair the incision to protect against infection."

"I know. It's okay, she has my younger brothers and sisters to care for. I will be fine."

Kat's heart went out to Pedro, bravely facing surgery without his mother being here to hold his hand, to kiss him and to wish him well. She could tell Miguel felt the same way, from the way his gaze softened as he looked down at Pedro.

"You are very brave, Pedro," Miguel murmured. "I am extremely proud of you."

The simple words brightened Pedro's face and he beamed up at Miguel as if he were some sort of miracle worker. She couldn't help wondering about Pedro's father, why he wasn't here if his mother was home with the other children.

Miguel oozed confidence and kindness at the same time. Obviously, he cared very much for children. First DiCarlo and now Pedro. Both were patients under his care, but she knew that was only part of it.

Miguel would be the same way with his own child. With Tommy. The truth was staring her in the face.

As they wheeled Pedro's bed down to the elevator to go to the surgical suite, she knew that she couldn't put off telling Miguel about his son for much longer. She didn't know if he still planned on keeping their dinner date, so much had happened since then.

But even if their dinner plans had to be cancelled, she would have to tell him. Tonight.

No more excuses.

# CHAPTER SIX

MIGUEL worked as quickly as he dared, first exploring the open wound in Pedro's abdomen and then irrigating with antibiotic solution. He believed the wound might have opened from a combination of an infection starting to take hold internally along with Pedro's physical exertions during the earthquake disaster.

He was lucky to have found an anesthesiology resident willing to stay after his shift. And Katerina was doing a phenomenal job of being his assistant. They settled into the old familiar routine as if the four and a half years hadn't gone by.

"Three-O silk," he said, but before he finished his statement Katerina was already handing him the pickups prepared with the suture. He grinned, even though she couldn't see behind the face mask, and gave his head a wry shake. "You always did have a way of reading my mind, Katerina."

She went still for a moment and he wondered if he'd somehow offended her. When she remained silent, he couldn't help trying to make amends.

"My apologies. I truly meant that as a compliment."

She lifted her head and looked at him, her beautiful green eyes probing as if she could indeed read his internal thoughts. "No apology necessary, Miguel," she finally said lightly. "I was thinking that I was glad that our roles weren't reversed and you were the one trying to read my mind."

"Really?" Closing the small incision didn't take long and he turned to face her as he set the pick-ups back down on the surgical tray. "Now you have piqued my interest. What is it you don't want me to read in your mind, I wonder?"

"Surely you don't expect me to answer that, do you?" Her green eyes crinkled at the corners, making him believe she was smiling. He relaxed, realizing he didn't like the thought of her being angry with him. "Pedro will be all right, won't he?"

"Yes, certainly. He must rest, though, and take care of himself. No more playing hero."

She nodded and there was a hint of relief in her gaze. "Good. That's very good."

She backed away from the surgical field and he had to bite back a protest, even though he knew her volunteer shift was over. Truly, she'd gone well above and beyond the call of duty. When she stripped off her face mask, he followed suit. "Katerina, I hope you will still allow me to take you to dinner this evening?"

She hesitated, and he sensed she wanted to refuse, but she surprised him by turning back to face him. "Of course, Miguel. But I need to return to my hotel for a bit. I'm still feeling the effects of jet-lag."

He couldn't blame her. The hour was still early, just three-thirty in the afternoon, and as much as he wanted to take her straight to his home, he couldn't begrudge her some down time. Especially not after everything she'd done for them today. "I will see you in a few hours, then?"

"Yes. I'll be ready." She glanced once more back at Pedro, where the anesthesiology resident was reversing the effects of his anesthesia, before she turned and disappeared through the doorway in the direction of the women's locker room.

He instantly felt isolated and alone after Katerina left, which was completely ridiculous. He stepped back, allowing the anesthesiologist to wheel Pedro's cart over to the recovery area.

As he washed up and changed his clothes, he spent time considering what meal he would prepare for her tonight. He wasn't a stranger to the kitchen. Living on his own, he'd been forced to learn how to cook, but he wanted to be sure the meal was to Katerina's liking.

For some odd reason he couldn't help feeling that tonight was incredibly important, a turning point in their renewed relationship.

And he was determined to make their evening together special.

"Mama!" Kat braced herself as her son launched himself at her, his chubby arms wrapping tightly around her neck.

"Oh, Tommy, I missed you so much!" She held him close, nuzzling his neck, filling her head with his scent, eternally grateful to have him in her life. The more difficult times of being a single mother were easily forgotten during joyous moments like this.

"We were just going to try and find something to

eat," Diana said with a tired smile. "I'm glad you came home before we left."

"I'm so hungry I could eat a bear," Kat murmured, still holding Tommy close. For once her active son seemed content to stay in her arms. "I'm surprised you didn't order room service."

"Can't read the room-service menu, it's in Spanish," Diana muttered with a heavy sigh. "Besides, we've been cooped up in here long enough. Believe it or not, there is a small café that's open just a few blocks away. We should be able to get something to eat. I have to tell you, the earthquake was a bit scary. There's one person behind the desk downstairs who speaks English and told us to stay in our rooms for a while. But I've been looking outside and haven't seen much damage."

Kat hadn't seen much evidence of damage either, and wondered if the tree outside the hospital had been partially dead already to have fallen on the building. "I'm so glad you're both safe."

"We're fine. We took a walk and found a couple of broken windows and a couple of uprooted trees. Nothing too awful."

"All right, let's go eat." She knew she had to tell Diana her plans for later that evening. But first she desperately needed something to eat. The gnawing in her stomach was almost painful.

While they ate, she explained how she'd helped out at the hospital in the children's ward, including doing surgery on a thirteen-year-old boy. As much as she didn't like being away from Tommy, she couldn't deny the satisfaction she'd felt by helping out.

"Hmm." Diana sat back in her seat, eyeing Kat over

the rim of her soft drink. "So basically you spent the entire day with Miguel, huh?"

Kat finished the *tapas* they'd ordered, not exactly sure what she was eating but enjoying the spicy food just the same, before answering. "Yes. And you may as well know I'm having dinner with him later tonight."

Her friend's eyes widened in horror. "No! You're going to tell him?"

"Don't," Kat said in warning, glancing at Tommy slurping his soft drink loudly through a straw. "Not now."

"But..." Diana sighed heavily, understanding that Kat didn't want to have this conversation with Tommy sitting right there. "I haven't had time to call the embassy," she complained in a low voice. "You agreed to wait."

"Doesn't matter." Kat was pleased to note how Tommy enjoyed the Spanish food. Must be part of his natural heritage, a trait passed down to him from Miguel. "Trust me when I tell you I know what I'm doing."

But Diana was shaking her head. "You don't know Miguel well enough yet," she protested.

"We worked together all day, moving the sick pediatric patients out of the children's wing. I helped him intubate a small child in the elevator and operate on a young boy. I know enough, Diana. You have to trust me on this."

Diana didn't say anything more, although the disapproval in her expression was clear. Even though Kat knew she was doing the right thing, she understood why her friend was worried. Seeing Miguel at the hospital today, there was no denying the powerful standing he had within the community, not to mention being on friendly terms with a police officer. A minor detail she hadn't dared tell Diana about. She hadn't understood exactly what they'd been saying, but when the police officer had taken Miguel's brother away, she'd had the impression he'd acted out of friendship.

But deep down those reasons weren't enough to hold her tongue. She knew Miguel was incapable of hurting a child, especially his own son. And he'd been so incredibly nice and supportive of her. Right from the very beginning, when he'd translated Juliet's chart for her. Spending time together today had only made her admire him more. No matter what Diana said, she would not back down from her decision.

Telling Miguel was the right thing to do.

"I hope you're not making a big mistake," Diana said.

"I'm not. Are you finished eating? We could take a little walk, maybe check out the church over there." Kat was determined to change the subject. She had a good hour yet before she needed to return to the hotel room to shower and change.

Better she keep her mind occupied with sightseeing rather than dwelling on the sweet anticipation of seeing Miguel again.

Kat pulled on the only dressy outfit she'd packed, a long gauzy skirt with a white tank top that molded to her figure. She left her long blonde hair straight and loose, rather than pulled back in the usual ponytail, knowing Miguel preferred it that way.

"You're dressing up for him as if this is some sort of hot date," Diana observed mildly.

She couldn't deny it. "Wanting to look nice isn't a crime." She needed some semblance of being in control. And maybe a part of her wanted to remind Miguel of the night they'd shared. A night of passion. A night that had produced a son.

Tommy was already falling asleep, and Kat couldn't help feeling guilty that she was leaving, forcing Diana to stay in the hotel room again. "I promise we'll do more sightseeing tomorrow," she said by way of apology.

"It's okay." Diana shrugged, even though Kat could sense her friend's keen disappointment. "This is why you paid my way to come here, right? There's no way we could have predicted the added complication of Miguel."

Truer words were never spoken. She went over to give her best friend a quick hug. "Thanks for being here, Diana."

Diana hugged her back, her good humor seeming to return. "You're welcome. Now, you'd better go downstairs, Miguel might just decide to come up here."

"He can't. They would make him call up here first," she protested. Still, she quickly crossed over to her half-asleep son, brushed a kiss on his brow and murmured how much she loved him before taking the room key Diana held out for her and letting herself out of the hotel room.

The elevators seemed to take for ever, but since she didn't know where the stairwells were, she forced herself to be patient. When the doors opened to reveal

Miguel standing there, she nearly screamed, her pulse leaping into triple digits.

"You scared me!" she accused, putting hand over her wildly beating heart. "What are you doing here?"

His teeth flashed in a bright smile, but he stood back, allowing her room to enter the elevator. "I'm sorry to have frightened you, but it's already five minutes past eight. I was worried you'd forgotten about our dinner date and had fallen asleep."

She struggled to breathe normally, but being in the small elevator so close to him was extremely nerve-racking. He was impeccably dressed in a crisp white shirt and black slacks, and his scent made her knees week. "How did you know what room I'm in? They're not supposed to tell you that. What if I didn't want to see you?" She was outraged that her privacy had been so easily violated.

"Hush, now, don't be so upset. The clerk at the front desk is one of my patients from the hospital. She knows I wouldn't hurt you."

As he spoke, the doubts Diana had voiced seeped into the back of her mind. Miguel knew everyone, had connections everywhere. He'd gotten her room number without any effort at all. What if he really did plan to take Tommy away from her?

She had to believe he wouldn't. But she wasn't willing to let him or the clerk off so lightly. "It's not right, Miguel. Just because she happens to know you, it doesn't mean she has the right to give you my room number. I intend to file a complaint."

He seemed taken aback by her biting anger. "I'm

sorry, Katerina. The fault is mine. Please don't get her in trouble for my mistake."

She knew she was overreacting, but the near miss had rattled her. What if he'd gotten a glimpse of Tommy? She didn't want him finding out about his son by accident. Back in the hotel room she'd been confident they could work something out, but now she wasn't so sure.

It was tempting to beg off their plans, but keeping Tommy a secret was already eating at her. She couldn't hold off another twenty-four hours, so she did her best to relax and smile. "Okay, fine, Miguel. I won't file a complaint, although you know I have a right to be upset. You forget I'm a single woman in a strange country where few speak my native language. I have a right to be concerned about strange men being allowed up to my room."

He lightly skimmed a hand down her back in a caress so light she thought she might have imagined it. "You are right, Katerina," he murmured contritely, although with a hint of steel. "I would not be at all happy if any other man was allowed access to your room."

The macho tone put her teeth on edge, but when the elevator doors opened she quickly escaped, putting badly needed distance between them.

She needed to stay in control. This wasn't a date, and she realized she'd made a grave mistake by dressing up for him as if it were. She was on an important mission, one that would have a great impact on her son's life, his future. Her future.

This was not a date!

* * *

Miguel cursed himself for being so stupid. If he'd been patient, they wouldn't be starting the night off on the wrong foot with an argument.

Katerina was breathtakingly beautiful. He'd never seen her in a dress and it was taking all his will-power to keep his hands to himself. He'd wanted to sweep her into his arms, to kiss her the way he had over four years ago.

His car was waiting, and he gently cupped her elbow, steering her towards the vehicle. Of course she dug in her heels. "I thought the restaurant was close by?"

"Please, get in the car. The restaurant nearby is closed due to the earthquake." After a brief pause she did as he asked, sliding into the back seat. "I'm afraid I have another sin to confess," he murmured, once they were settled and the driver had pulled away from the curb.

Her brows pulled together in a frown. "Really? And what sin is that?"

He subtly wiped his damp palms on his pants, more nervous than he'd ever been in his life. He was used to women coming on to him, many made it no secret they wanted to be the one to help end his bachelor ways. But he suddenly cared what Katerina thought of him. It was telling that she hugged the door as if she might escape at any moment. He flashed his most charming smile. "I have made dinner for us tonight."

"You?" her eyebrows shot upwards in surprise. And then the full meaning sank in. "We're going to your home?"

She acted as if he intended to take advantage of her. Had he read her wrong? Was it possible that she didn't feel the same sexual awareness that he did? Or had his stupid stunt in going up to her room broken her trust? "If you'd rather not, we can wait until tomorrow to dine. Hopefully the restaurants will reopen by then. I'm more than willing to ask my driver to return to your hotel." He tried not to let his hurt feelings show.

There was a long pause before she let out a small sigh. "No need to go back, Miguel," she said softly. She lifted her gaze and he saw the faint glint of amusement there. "I must say, I'm stunned to learn you know how to cook."

He relaxed and lifted her hand to his mouth, pressing his mouth to her soft skin. "There are many things you don't know about me, Katerina."

She gasped and tugged on her hand, which he reluctantly released. "And maybe, Miguel, there are a few things you don't know about me."

He couldn't deny the burning need to get to know all her secrets. The driver pulled up to his home and she glanced out the window. "You live right by the hospital," she said, recognizing the landmarks.

"Yes, very convenient for those nights I'm on call," he agreed.

His home was on the top floor, and they rode the elevator up in silence. He unlocked the door and then stepped back, allowing Katerina to enter first.

"Wow, very nice," she murmured, and he was ridiculously pleased she liked his home. "Bigger than I expected for a man living alone."

She didn't sit, but wandered around looking at his things with interest. When she approached the hallway farthest from the kitchen, he said, "Feel free to explore.

There are three bedrooms, although our rooms tend to be smaller than you're used to back in the U.S."

He turned to check on the food, which was being kept warm in the oven, and when he turned around he was startled to find her standing right behind him.

She was so beautiful, he ached. "Katerina, please don't be angry with me." He stepped closer, reaching up to thread his fingers through the silky golden strands of her hair. "I wanted tonight to be special."

A strange expression, something akin to guilt, flashed in her eyes, but then she smiled and he knew he was forgiven. "I'm not angry," she murmured.

"I don't think I've thanked you properly for your help today," he murmured, moving closer still. She stared up at him, standing her ground, and he couldn't resist the soft invitation of her mouth for another minute. Without giving her a chance to say anything more, he gently cupped her face in his hands and kissed her.

## CHAPTER SEVEN

KAT didn't know how she allowed it to happen but the instant Miguel kissed her, memories of the night they'd shared came rushing back to her, flooding her mind, making her melt against him. Instinctively, she opened her mouth, wordlessly inviting him to deepen the kiss.

One moment his mouth was gentle, the next it was demanding, needy, stirring up flames of desire she'd tried to forget, vowed to live without.

She'd missed this. Missed him. Missed the way he made her feel, alive, vibrant, attractive. She wrapped her arms tightly around his neck, hanging on for dear life as a storm of desire washed over her, nearly drowning her with its intensity.

"Katerina," he whispered, as he pressed soft, moist kisses down the side of her neck. "You are so beautiful to me. I've never forgotten you. Never."

For one long moment she almost gave in to his sinful temptation. His hand came up to gently cup her breast, his thumb stroking her nipple through the thin layer of cotton, and her body reacted, arching into his, desperately needing to feel his hands on her bare skin.

She wanted nothing more than to close her eyes and give in to the whisper of pure pleasure, but she wasn't that younger, carefree person any more. She was a single mother with responsibilities.

Appalled with herself, she quickly broke off the embrace, forcing herself to let Miguel go, stumbling in her haste to put the width of the kitchen table between them. She grasped the back of a chair so tightly her knuckles were white. "I'm sorry, but I can't do this. I didn't come here to—to pick up where we left off, Miguel."

She couldn't allow the flash of hurt in his eyes to get to her. Too bad if his macho pride had taken a low blow. He would survive. She had to think about Tommy now. She watched him struggle to pull himself under control and she was a little ashamed of herself for being glad he'd been as aroused as she had been. At least she knew for sure the attraction wasn't one-sided.

"Of course you didn't," he said slowly, as if articulating each word helped him to maintain control. "I promised you dinner and I always follow through on my promises."

Dinner? Food? He had to be joking. She couldn't have eaten a bite to save her life. She shook her head and took a long deep breath, before letting it out slowly. "Miguel, listen to me. I came here because I have something to tell you. Something very important." She forced herself to meet his gaze.

He seemed truly baffled and took a step towards her, and she instinctively took a quick step back. "What is it, Katerina? Are you all right? It's not...your health, is it?"

She couldn't help being touched that he cared enough to worry about her health. And if she was sick, would he stand by her? Or would he look for an excuse to leave?

She didn't want to consider the answer to that question, so she ruthlessly shoved the thought aside.

Obviously, he wasn't going to be able to figure this out on his own. She'd have to come right out to say it. "I'm fine, Miguel. But there is something you should know." She took a deep breath and bravely faced him. "I have a son. *We* have a son. He will be four years old in a little less than three months."

He gaped at her in shock, and for several long seconds the silence was heavy between them. She wished she could read his mind to know what he was thinking. "A son?" he echoed, almost in disbelief.

"His name is Tomas. I named him after you." During the night they'd shared, Miguel had confided that Tomas was his middle name. And his father's name.

Miguel dragged a hand down his face, as if still hardly able to comprehend what she was saying. "I don't understand. How did this happen? We used protection."

She batted down the flicker of anger—hadn't she asked herself the same question while staring down at the positive pregnancy test? But having him think, even for a moment, that she might have done this on purpose made her grind her teeth in frustration. "Protection can fail, Miguel. I'm sorry to spring this on you so suddenly. You need to know I tried to find you after you left. I called your cellphone and searched for you on all the popular social media websites. When I couldn't find you, I assumed you were working somewhere remote with Doctors Without Borders, following your dream." She spread her hands wide. "I didn't know Seville was your home. Had no way of knowing you were here all this time."

Miguel looked in shock and he lowered himself slowly onto a kitchen chair. "A son. Tomas. I can barely comprehend what you are telling me."

Relieved to have the secret out in the open, she sank into a chair across from him and reached for her purse. "I have a picture. Would you like to see?" Without waiting for his reply, she slid Tommy's picture across the table. "He looks very much like you, Miguel."

He stared at the glossy photograph for several long moments before he dragged his gaze up to meet hers. "This is such a shock. I don't know what to say, other than that he's amazing. Thank you for bearing him."

There had really been no choice, not for her. The way Miguel stared at the picture, as if awestruck, made her a bit nervous. Was he already thinking of taking their son away from her? Beneath the table she linked her fingers together, tightly. "Miguel, I only told you about Tommy because you had a right to know. Please be assured, I'm more than capable of raising him. I don't expect anything from you."

For the first time since arriving in Spain she saw his gaze darken with anger directed at her. "I will not avoid my responsibility, Katerina," he murmured in a low tone. For just a brief moment she thought he looked upset, but then the fleeting expression was gone. In its place was grim resolution. "Of course I will provide for my son. And I would like to make arrangements to meet him. As soon as possible. I know Juliet will be here for a few more days, but I can make arrangements for the two of us to return immediately to the U.S."

She stared at him, realizing in some portion of her brain that Miguel didn't know Tommy was here in

Seville with her. Was, in fact, sleeping soundly back in her hotel room. If she told Miguel he was there, she had no doubt he'd swoop in and wake him up, scaring the poor child to death. She strove to keep her tone level. "Miguel, be reasonable. He's a young boy, not yet four. He won't understand or recognize you. You will be a stranger to him. We need some time to think this through, to figure out what we're going to do. Besides, I don't want to leave Juliet yet."

Miguel slowly rose to his feet, staring down at her arrogantly. "If you think I will let you raise my son without me, you are sorely mistaken. I will be a part of his life, and nothing you do or say will change my mind."

The sick feeling in her stomach intensified as she stared up at him helplessly, knowing he meant every single word. And while she knew she'd have to share custody of Tommy with Miguel, she wasn't at all sure what that exactly meant regarding their future.

Would Miguel play at being a father at first but then lose interest in them? Would he decide to up and leave, just like her father had? The way Juliet's father had?

Seeing him with Pedro earlier, she'd thought Miguel would be a good father to her son. But now she couldn't prevent the doubts from seeping in. And she desperately needed time. Needed to understand exactly what the future truly held for them.

How much would she have to sacrifice for her son?

Miguel inwardly winced when Katerina eyes filled with wounded shock. He knew he'd crossed the line, had put her on the defensive by practically threatening her, but he couldn't seem to stop.

She'd borne his son. Had been raising him alone for years. Deep down he was outraged that he had been cheated of precious memories, yet logically he knew the situation wasn't her fault. He'd left to return home after his father's stroke, leaving Katerina to fend for herself. He'd simply assumed she'd be fine. Bitter guilt for not talking to her again after he'd left coated his tongue. She'd had every right to believe he was working in some distant country—after all, he'd told her about his dream. And truthfully, if not for his brother's drinking problem, he would have already been in Africa, working with those in need. He wouldn't be here now, hearing the truth about having a son. And she'd searched for him, too.

For a moment his resolve wavered. For so long he'd dreamed of joining Doctors Without Borders. Now his dream would have to be put on hold once again. Indefinitely. Maybe for ever.

He squelched the feeling of despair and refused to allow himself to think about that now. Instead, he glanced once more at the glossy photograph of a young boy with light brown skin, dark hair, and big dark eyes. His bright smile was the only facial feature that resembled Katerina. He trailed his fingertips over the photo and had the strongest urge to hop onto the first plane to the U.S. to see Tomas in person.

"Miguel? I smell something burning," Katerina said in a tight voice.

He whirled around in surprise, having totally forgotten about the meal he'd prepared. He went over to pull the chicken dish from the oven, waving the smoke away. "I don't think it's too badly burned," he said, even though the chicken looked a bit on the overdone side.

"I'm not hungry," Katerina murmured. She pushed away from the table and rose to her feet. "I think it's best that I go back to the hotel now. We can discuss this more tomorrow."

He swung around to face her, unwilling to call an abrupt end to their evening. "Don't leave," he said, his voice sharply commanding rather than pleading with her, the way he should. He forced himself to soften his tone. "If you could spare a few minutes, I would like to hear more about Tomas."

She stood indecisively, wringing her hands together, and he silently cursed himself for being so stupid. He'd frightened her, instead of reassuring her that he intended to be there for her and for Tomas. Maybe a part of him mourned the loss of his dream, but he refused, absolutely refused, to ignore his responsibilities.

He'd been selfish once, following his dream to study abroad, and his brother Luis had suffered for it. His father had suffered too. He would always regret not being there when his father had sustained his stroke. The fact that he'd saved countless patients' lives wasn't enough to make up for his failures regarding his family.

He couldn't bear to fail his son.

"There isn't much to tell," she protested. "He's hardly more than a baby."

Katerina avoided his direct gaze and he wished he could cross over and take her once again into his arms. Kissing her had felt like heaven and he'd nearly lost all control when she'd wantonly kissed him back.

"He's not stubborn, like his mother?" he asked, trying to lighten the mood by gently teasing her. "I find that difficult to believe."

She narrowed her gaze and flipped her long golden hair over her shoulder. "Believe me, Tommy gets his stubborn streak from his father."

He tried not to wince at the shortened version of his son's name. He didn't understand this American tendency to give nicknames rather than using given names. "I bet he's smart, then, too. Just like me."

Katerina rolled her eyes. "Of course he's smart. I read to him before he goes to bed at night and he has memorized every story. He attends preschool and already knows his letters and numbers."

Hearing about his son's life, bedtime stories and preschool caused helpless anger to wash over him. He'd missed so much. Too much.

She was right, his son didn't know him. He couldn't bear the thought of being a stranger to his own son. "I can't wait to see him, Katerina. I want to see him, to hold him in my arms. I feel like I've missed too much already."

Her expression went from tolerant amusement to frank alarm. "Miguel, you can't just barge into his life like a steamroller. You'll be a stranger to him. You have to give him time to get to know you. And what exactly are you suggesting? That we'll just move here to Seville to be near you? Neither one of us speaks the language here and, besides, Tommy is an American citizen. We have a life back home." As she spoke, Katerina edged closer to the door, her eyes wide with panic.

"I'm sorry, but this is too much stress for me to handle right now, Miguel. I came to Seville because of

Juliet's injuries, remember? And after working all day, I can barely think straight. We'll talk tomorrow."

"Katerina..." he protested, but too late. She already had her hand on the front door. He knew he was pushing her too hard, too fast. "All right. We can talk more tomorrow. I'll be happy to take you back to the hotel."

"I'll ride the metro," she said, lifting her chin in the stubborn gesture he secretly found amusing. Except that her eagerness to get away from him wasn't at all comical.

"Katerina, please allow me to take you." When she still looked like a rabbit ready to bolt, he added, "If you insist on taking the metro, I will have no choice but to follow you. We will ride together."

Her mouth tightened, but after a moment she gave a small, jerky nod. "Fine. We'll take your car. But I'd like to go now, Miguel."

He couldn't think of a way to talk her out of it, so he simply nodded and reached for his cellphone. He called his driver, Fernando, and requested him to return right away. Fernando sounded surprised, but readily agreed. "My driver will be here in five minutes," he assured her.

Katerina didn't move away from the door, but simply looked at him from across the room, a long awkward silence stretching between them. He glanced over at the photograph of Tomas, still sitting on the kitchen table. "May I keep the picture of my son?" he asked in a low voice.

For a moment he thought Katerina was going to burst into tears, but she bit her lip and nodded. "Of course," she murmured in a husky voice. "I have others at home."

The way she said the word home, as if he wasn't included, made his temper flare, but he managed to hold his tongue. Thankfully, Fernando arrived quicker than expected.

Katerina didn't say more than a couple brief sentences on the way back to her hotel. He couldn't think of anything to say to put her mind at ease. Because even though he didn't want to upset her, there was no way on earth he was going to give his son up easily.

"Thank you for the ride," she said politely, when Fernando pulled up in front of her hotel. "I'm sure I'll see you some time tomorrow."

He caught her hand before she escaped from the car. "Katerina, wait. How about if we agree to meet at eleven o'clock tomorrow morning? I will have finished making rounds by then. We'll meet in your sister's room and then we can go somewhere for a cup of coffee, okay?"

"Fine. I'll see you at eleven." She looked pointedly down at where his hand was locked around her wrist and he forced himself to let her go. "Goodnight," she said, and didn't wait for him to respond before slamming the door shut and practically sprinting into the lobby.

He watched her hurry away, trying not to panic at the realization that she could easily catch a flight home tonight, making it extremely difficult for him to find her. And his son.

"Ready, sir?" Fernando asked from the front seat.

He hesitated, fighting the urge to follow her upstairs to her hotel room before she could slip away, maybe for ever. He wanted to talk to her about how they would deal with this situation, to insist they finish their conversation right this minute.

He took several deep breaths, fighting to stay calm.

Logically, he knew Katerina wasn't going to run away. She wouldn't leave Juliet, not when her sister had suffered seizures earlier that afternoon. Besides, no one had forced her to tell him about his son. Truthfully, Katerina could have kept Tomas a secret, simply returning home without telling him a thing. The fact that she had told him indicated she wanted their son to have a father. The thought calmed him.

"Yes, I'm ready, Fernando," he said, giving his driver the signal to leave. As they pulled away from the curb and headed home, Miguel sat back in his seat, his mind whirling.

He had until tomorrow morning at eleven to come up with a new plan. He needed some way to convince Katerina that Tommy would benefit from having them all be together as a family, rather than living apart. Surely she wanted such a thing as well, or she wouldn't have told him her secret.

Granted, the obstacle of living in different countries was no small thing. They both had family members to take into consideration as well. He had his brother Luis, who still needed support, and she had Juliet, who might need ongoing medical care.

The entire situation seemed impossible, but he was determined there would be a way to make things work out to everyone's satisfaction.

Grimly, he stared out through the night, knowing he would fight anyone and anything that stood in the way of establishing a relationship with his son.

## CHAPTER EIGHT

K AT barely made it up to her hotel room where she collapsed in the chair beside the bed and buried her face in her hands, trying not to give in to mounting hysteria.

Miguel wanted to meet his son, and it sounded pretty certain that he would want custody. All this time she'd figured he wouldn't want the responsibility of having a family, yet he'd made it clear that he intended to follow her back to the U.S. in order to claim Tommy as his own.

"Kat?" Diana whispered from the bed. "Are you all right?"

She lifted her head and struggled to swallow her tears. Thankfully, Tommy was sleeping in the small roll-away bed as he would only be upset to see her crying. The room was dark, but they always left the bathroom light on in case Tommy needed to get up. "Fine," she whispered back, subtly swiping her hands over her wet cheeks. "We'll talk in the morning."

She wished Diana was asleep already too, because her emotions were too raw, too fragile to talk now.

Maybe Diana had been right to encourage her to wait before telling Miguel about Tommy. She wished she'd listened to her friend's advice. But it was too late now.

There was nothing to do except to move forward from here. Telling Miguel about his son was the right thing to do, but while she thought she'd prepared herself for the conversation, Miguel's reaction had overwhelmed her.

He'd assumed she'd left her son back home, and she hadn't possessed the courage to tell him otherwise. She could rationalize the reason was because Miguel would have come right up here to the room, demanding to see Tommy regardless of the fact that he was already asleep. Regardless of the fact that seeing a stranger might upset him.

But deep down she knew her reasons for keeping silent were far more selfish. She'd needed a little time to come to grips with how her life would change from this point on. Miguel's demand to return immediately to the U.S. had frightened her. The fantasy she'd harbored, where Miguel would allow her to continue to raise his son while he joined Doctors Without Borders, had exploded in her face.

She crept over to the side of the roll-away bed where Tommy was sleeping to gaze down at his sweet, innocent face. He was clutching his favorite stuffed animal, Terry the tiger, to his chest. She lightly brushed her fingers over his silky dark hair, being careful not to wake him up. She wanted to gather him close into her arms, as if to reassure herself that she wasn't going to lose him.

She pressed a soft kiss to the top of his head, before heading into the bathroom to wash her face and change into her nightgown. She crawled into her bed and stared blindly up at the ceiling, knowing she'd never relax enough to fall asleep.

Going back over the events of the evening, she

couldn't help remembering, in vivid detail, the way Miguel had kissed her. Before he'd known about Tommy. He'd clearly wanted her, his body's reaction had been no secret. Had he assumed that since they'd made love four and a half years ago she wouldn't think twice about doing so again?

It had been tempting, far more tempting that she wanted to admit, to give in to the passion that shimmered between them. Truthfully, Tommy was the main reason she'd pulled back. If not for her son, she knew that she and Miguel would have continued where they'd left off all those years ago.

Because she cared about Miguel. More than she should. And while they might be able to get along enough to share custody of their son, she wasn't sure how to get past her personal feelings for him.

"Mama, wake up!" Tommy said, climbing up on her bed. "I'm hungry."

Kat forced her gritty eyelids open, inwardly groaning. She'd been awake half the night, worrying herself sick about the future, and could easily have slept for several more hours. But as a parent she was used to putting her needs aside for her son. "I'm awake," she murmured, trying to focus on the clock across the room and wincing when she realized it was seven a.m.

"Do you want me to take Tommy down to the café for breakfast?" Diana asked as she came out of the bathroom. "You can probably catch another hour or so of sleep."

"No, that's fine. I want to come with you." Kat sat up, running her fingers through her hair. "I was thinking maybe we should go on the boat tour this morning, instead of waiting until later."

Diana's eyes lit up. "That would be great."

Kat didn't have the heart to tell her friend that by early afternoon she'd likely be arranging a meeting between Miguel and Tommy. Better to put that conversation off for a little while yet. "Give me fifteen minutes to get ready, okay?"

"Sure."

Kat freshened up in the bathroom, forgoing a shower to pull her hair back into its usual ponytail. During the long night, when she'd tossed and turned for hours, she'd decided Tommy needed his father, so she planned to present Miguel with her joint custody proposal. As much as it pained her, she thought that having Tommy spend summers here with Miguel, along with a few holidays, would probably be the least disruptive to their lives. And she could travel with Tommy to make sure things went well, at least for the first few years. She could only hope that Miguel would find parenting too much work. Although remembering the way he cared for the pediatric patients in the hospital, like Pedro and DiCarlo, she knew he wouldn't.

Tommy ran into the bathroom and grabbed her hand. "Mama, let's go."

"All right, all right. Slow down. Diana, do you have your room key?"

"Right here." Diana held it up.

"All right, here's mine. After we go on the boat ride, I'm going to head over to the hospital to see Juliet." And Miguel, although she didn't voice that last part.

"Do you want to stop on the way?" Diana offered.

She did, very much, but at the same time she was too afraid they'd run into Miguel. And since she'd promised Diana and Tommy a boat ride, she was determined to follow through on her promise. If she was back in the U.S., she could simply call the hospital to see how her sister was doing, but with the language barrier she had no choice but to actually go in to see Juliet for herself. And it didn't help that Miguel's eleven o'clock time frame hung over her head like a time bomb. "No, that's okay. Let's do the boat tour first."

As they left the hotel and walked down the street to their favorite breakfast café, she was determined to have this short time to play tourist with Diana and Tommy. A few hours alone, before their lives changed, for ever.

"Look at these bikes, Kat—isn't this the coolest idea?" Diana said as she gestured toward the bike rack located a few feet from the café. "I found out that this is a type of public transportation offered in Seville. For a small annual fee you can take one of these bikes, ride it to your destination, park it in another bike rack and then use it again to go home. No need to buy a bike of your own. These bike racks and bikes are located all over the city."

Kat smiled when she saw an elderly gentleman ride away on one of the red and white bikes, his front basket full of groceries. "Very cool idea."

"Have you notice the people walk or bike everywhere? No wonder they're healthier than Americans." Diana was starting to sound like a TV commercial sprouting the benefits of living in Seville.

"Remember, this is southern Spain where the weather

is mild and we live in the northeast of the U.S. Biking in snow and ice isn't an easy task."

"Maybe," Diana murmured. "But I have to say, this trip has really opened my eyes to how other cultures thrive."

Kat couldn't disagree. They finished their breakfast and took the metro to the heart of the city, where the sidewalk vendors sold tickets for the boat tours. Tommy was happy to be on the move, running from one location to the other. She gave him room to run, knowing that his boundless energy had to be let loose some time.

They had to wait almost thirty minutes for the next tour, and Kat kept an eye on the time, knowing she needed to head back to the hospital in order to meet Miguel by eleven o'clock. As much as she wanted to enjoy the tour, her stomach was knotted with nerves.

The boat tour wasn't crowded this early in the morning and they had almost the entire upper deck of the boat to themselves. Tommy was thrilled when she lifted him up so that he could see over the railing.

The tour lasted almost an hour, and by the time they disembarked from the boat Kat knew they needed to head back toward the hotel. "No, we need to go this way, Tommy," she called, when he took off down the sidewalk.

Her son ignored her instruction and Diana glanced at her. "I'll get him," she offered.

"No, I'll go." Kat took off after Tommy, who was running and laughing as if they were playing a game of chase. She wanted to be mad at him, but just listening to him laugh made her smile. She gained on him and tried to get his attention. "Tommy, come on, now. We have to go for a ride on the metro."

A woman walking a dog was heading towards them and Tommy suddenly swerved right in front of them. The dog was on a leash but reacted instinctively by jumping up and nipping at him at the same time both Kat and the dog's owner shouted, "No!"

Tommy let out a wail as the dog's owner yanked the dog back and Kat rushed over, picking Tommy up and carrying him out of harm's way. "Shh, it's okay. You're okay, Tommy," she crooned as she tried to examine him for injuries.

Her heart sank when she found puncture marks in the fleshy part of Tommy's arm a few inches above the wrist. The wounds were bleeding, and she glanced up as Diana joined them, feeling like the worst mother on the planet. "The dog bit him."

Diana was a nurse too, and she looked at the wounds with a grimace. "We need to get that cleaned up right away."

"Yeah, but I think he'll need antibiotics too. Do they have clinics here? Or should we go straight to the hospital?" She hated knowing this was all her fault. She shouldn't have let Tommy run around. She should have anticipated something like this.

The dog owner was talking in rapid Spanish, clearly upset about what happened. Kat tried to smile, shaking her head. *"No comprendo Espanol,"* she said.

"They must have clinics," Diana was saying with a frown. But Kat had already made up her mind.

"We'll go to the hospital where Juliet is being cared for. I saw an emergency department there."

"Are you sure that's a good idea?" Diana asked. "We could run into Miguel."

"It's a risk, but Tommy needs good medical care. Miguel is a surgeon—chances are good that we'll be in and out of there without him knowing." And even if they weren't, she wasn't going to worry about Miguel's reaction at seeing them. Tommy's health was far more important.

Diana reluctantly agreed. Kat made sure they stopped in a restroom to wash the dog bite with soap and water, before taking the metro back to the hospital. As they walked into the small emergency room, Kat couldn't help glancing around for any sign of Miguel.

Tommy was, of course, her first concern. Miguel already knew about their son, but she didn't really want him to find out like this that Tommy was here in Seville. She would much rather tell him herself.

The woman at the desk in the emergency room didn't speak any English, and she showed her the dog bite on Tommy's arm, pulling out her Spanish dictionary to find the word for dog. *"Perro,"* she said, demonstrating the action of biting.

*"Sí, un momento."* The woman spoke to someone else in Spanish, and then took them back to a small exam room. Kat was glad to see the nurse bring in a wash basin.

She relaxed, feeling better now that they were actually getting medical care for Tommy. She glanced at her watch, realizing she was going to be late for her meeting with Miguel.

"I can stay with Tommy if you need me to," Diana offered, sensing her distress.

She slowly shook her head. "No, I can't just leave. Not until I know the wound is clean and that he'll get the antibiotics he needs."

If she had a way to call Miguel, she would. But as she didn't, she could only hope Miguel would have patience and wait for her.

Miguel arrived at the hospital early, unable to contain his excitement. He'd found a flight to Cambridge that was scheduled to leave early the next morning and he'd been tempted to go ahead and book it, except that he wasn't sure when Katerina's return flight was scheduled for. It wouldn't help him to get there before she arrived. Yet he was thrilled that he was closer than ever to meeting his son.

He went up to see how Juliet was doing, hoping that she would soon be stable enough to transfer home. He was pleased to discover that she was following instructions again and hadn't had any more seizures. Her electrolytes were back to normal, which was also a very good sign. He left orders to begin weaning her from the ventilator.

She wasn't quite ready for transfer back home but would be soon.

Since he was early, he decided to check on his other patients. First he checked on DiCarlo, who remained in the I.C.U. The boy was still critical, but his vitals were stable. From there, he headed over to the temporary children's ward to visit with Pedro.

"Hi, Dr. Vasquez," Pedro greeted him. The boy looked a little better, although still a little too pale and drawn. He didn't like seeing the dark circles beneath Pedro's eyes.

"Pedro, how are you feeling?" He crossed the room and checked the nursing notes on the clipboard. "Why aren't you taking pain medication?"

Pedro grimaced. "I don't like the way they make me feel."

"Maybe not, but I don't think you're getting enough rest. Sleep is very important. You will heal much faster if you take some pain medication at nighttime."

The boy flashed a wan smile. "You sound like Miss Kat. That same thing she explained to me yesterday."

Miguel nodded, sensing a bit of puppy love for Katerina in Pedro's gaze. "Katerina is a very smart lady. You would do well to follow her advice."

Pedro was quiet for a moment. "I thought she might come to visit me today."

He saw the stab of disappointment in the boy's eyes. "She is planning to come later, and I'm sure she will visit. I'll need to talk to your mother about keeping you here another day, Pedro."

"She won't care. She is too busy at home with my brothers and sisters."

Miguel wished there was something he could say to make the boy feel better. "That may be true, but you also help her, don't you? I'm sure she misses you."

"Of course." Pedro winced as he shifted in the bed. He put a tentative hand over his incision. "But I don't think carrying my brothers and sisters is a good idea right now."

"No, that would not be good," Miguel agreed. He lifted Pedro's hospital gown and gently peeled back the gauze dressing to examine his wound. The skin around the incision was a little red and he gently palpated the area to make sure there was no pus beneath the skin. There wasn't, but he decided to add yet another antibiotic just to be on the safe side. The risk of infection was high. "Looks good, but you have to take your pain medications. I need you to get up and walk the hallways. Staying in bed all day isn't healthy."

Pedro nodded. "Okay, I will do that."

Miguel called for the nurse and waited until Pedro had taken the ordered pain medication before he moved on to the next patient. He took his time making rounds, wanting to be sure to have everything finished before he spent time with Katerina.

He returned to Juliet's room at exactly eleven o'clock, frowning when he discovered Katerina hadn't arrived yet. He went back out to the nurses' station. "Has Juliet's sister been here to visit?" he asked in Spanish.

"No, Dr. Vasquez, she has not been here yet."

He gave a brief nod, hiding his impatience. He went back to DiCarlo's room, reviewing the chart to make sure his orders had been carried out, secretly watching for Katerina to arrive.

At eleven-thirty his temper began to simmer. Was it possible his worst fears had been realized? That she'd actually taken an earlier flight home in an attempt to hide Tomas from him? He didn't want to believe she would do such a thing, but as the minutes passed with agonizing slowness, he couldn't help believing the worst.

At noon he muttered an oath and left the hospital, calling his driver to take him to Katerina's hotel. He had to know she was still here in Seville. And if she was simply trying to avoid him, he would make certain she never did such a thing ever again.

His driver pulled up in front of the hotel and Fernando had barely put the car in park before Miguel shot out of the back seat, striding purposefully up to the front desk. "I need to speak with Katerina Richardson in room 212," he said.

"I will ring the room," the clerk said. After a few minutes he shrugged and hung up. "I'm afraid there is no answer."

"But she's still a guest here, right?" Miguel persisted. The time was almost twelve-thirty and most of the flights back to the U.S. left early in the morning, but there had been one early-afternoon flight.

"*Sí, señor,* she is still a guest. If you would like to wait, I suggest you have a seat in the lobby."

Miguel was too keyed up to sit in the lobby so he went back outside to let Fernando know he'd be staying for a while. He paced back and forth for several minutes, before taking a seat in the outside café adjacent to the hotel. He ordered a soft drink, although he was in the mood for something far stronger.

Within minutes a familiar voice reached his ears. "Walk, Tommy, don't run. Here, take my hand."

He went still, hardly able to believe his ears. Tommy? Slowly he turned in his seat in time to see Katerina walking up the sidewalk toward the hotel, holding the hand of a young boy.

The same boy in the photograph she'd given him.
*Their son!*

## CHAPTER NINE

MIGUEL slowly rose to his feet, his anger towards Katerina fading as he drank in the sight of his son. Seeing Tomas in person was so much better than a photograph. The boy was so animated, Miguel could barely breathe.

Katerina abruptly stopped in her tracks, going pale when her gaze locked on his. But then she took a deep breath and said something in a low voice to her companion, a woman with dark hair who looked vaguely familiar, as she resumed walking.

He wanted to rush over and sweep his son into his arms, but remembering what Katerina had said yesterday about how he was a stranger to Tomas, it gave him the strength to stay right where he was. It wasn't until Katerina and Tomas came closer that he noticed the white gauze dressing on his son's left forearm.

"Hi, Miguel," she greeted him. "I'm sorry I missed you at the hospital. This is my son, Tommy, who had a small accident. And you remember my friend, Diana Baylor?"

He cleared his throat, striving to play along as if seeing his son in person hadn't completely knocked him off balance. "Of course I remember. Diana, it's good to see

you again. And this is your son, Tommy?" He purposefully used Katerina's dreadful nickname and crouched
down so he was at eye level with the child and wouldn't
seem so intimidating. "Hi, Tommy, my name is Miguel
Vasquez. I'm very happy to meet you."

Tomas stared at him with his large brown eyes and
shrank back toward his mother, as if suddenly shy.
Miguel didn't want to frighten the boy, but at the same
time he couldn't help being frustrated that his son didn't
know him.

He had to remind himself that the situation was his
own fault. Not Katerina's. And certainly not the child's.

"It's okay, Tommy," Katerina said, brushing a hand
over his dark hair. "Miguel is a good friend of mine.
Show him where the dog bit you on the arm."

Tomas held out his arm, the one covered in gauze.
"Bad doggy bit me," he said solemnly.

"Tommy, remember how you ran straight at the
doggy? He only nipped at you because he was scared,"
Katerina said, filling in the gaps of what had happened
for Miguel. "And the emergency-room nurse gave you
a lollipop, didn't she?"

There was a hint of red staining the child's fingers
and teeth as he nodded vigorously. "I'm a good boy."

"I'm sure you were a very good boy," Miguel said
with a smile, relieved to know that his son had received
appropriate medical care for the dog bite. Obviously,
this was the reason Katerina hadn't met him in her sister's room. A very good excuse, except that it didn't at
all explain why she'd let him believe Tomas was back
in the U.S.

Although he'd assumed that, hadn't he? Katerina hadn't lied to him, but she had withheld the truth.

He would grant her a pass on this one, but now that she was here, with Tomas, he was determined to spend as much time with his son as possible.

And Katerina had better not try to stand in his way.

Kat had been shocked to find Miguel waiting for her outside their hotel, but by the time she noticed him it was too late as he'd already recognized Tommy. At least now there were no more secrets. She could see Miguel wasn't happy with her, but there wasn't much she could do. This had already been a rough day, and it was barely one o'clock in the afternoon.

"Katerina, do you think the three of us could take a walk?" Miguel asked, as he rose to his feet. "No offense, Diana, but I'd like some time alone with Katerina and Tomas."

Diana crossed her arms over her chest and shrugged, glancing over at her. "Kat? What would you like to do?"

Kat knew her friend would stand by her, if asked, but she'd known that Miguel would want to spend time with his son and there was no good reason to delay. "We'll be fine, Diana. You deserve some down time anyway. Should we meet back here at the hotel in an hour or so? Tommy will be more than ready for his nap by then."

"Sure thing." Diana's gaze was full of suspicion as she glanced over at Miguel. "Nice meeting you again, Dr. Vasquez," she said politely, before turning to walk away.

"I'm getting the sense she doesn't like me very

much," Miguel murmured after Diana was out of earshot.

"Diana has always been there for me when I needed her. She was my labor coach and has helped me out more times than I could count, especially on days when I needed child care when Tommy was sick." Her temper flared. She was unwilling to allow him to put down her friend.

Miguel winced as her barb hit home. "In other words, she blames me for not being there with you."

Kat glanced down at Tommy and decided this wasn't the time or the place to argue about the past. "You wanted to take a walk, so let's walk. There's a park not far from here, down the block and across the street."

Miguel nodded and fell into step beside her, keeping Tommy between them. "Yes, I played at that park often as a young boy. See that school there?" He gestured toward the white building across the street. "That's where both my brother and I attended school."

She remembered seeing the young kids all wearing their navy blue and white plaid uniforms running outside at recess. Today was Sunday, so there weren't any children playing now, but she couldn't help wondering if Miguel was insinuating that he wanted Tommy to attend the same school he had. She struggled to remain calm. "Yes, I saw the students playing outside in their uniforms the other day. I was struck by how similar the school was to ours back home."

"Tommy, do you like school?" Miguel asked, turning his attention to their son.

"Yeah." Tommy seemed to be slowly warming up to Miguel. "School is fun."

"Do you play games at school?" Miguel persisted.

"Yep. I play with my friends."

Kat couldn't help smiling as Miguel tried to have a conversation with their son. Too bad that having a rational conversation with an almost four-year-old wasn't easy. Miguel was lucky to get anything more than one- or two-word answers to his questions.

When they reached the park Tommy tugged on her hand so she let him go, allowing him to run over to the water fountain. He looked over the cement edge, peering into the water.

"I can't believe you didn't tell me he was here," Miguel said in a low tone. "Do you realize I almost booked a flight to Cambridge this morning?"

"I'm sorry, Miguel. But Tommy was already asleep and I couldn't risk you marching into the room and waking him up. Besides, I honestly planned on bringing him with me to see you today. Unfortunately Tommy's dog bite prevented me from meeting you at the hospital, as we'd planned."

He sensed the truth in her words and forced himself to relax.

"But why would you book a flight without discussing your plans with me?" she continued. "You can't bulldoze your way into Tommy's life, Miguel. What we want doesn't matter here. The only thing that matters is what's best for Tommy." She turned to face him. "I told you about our son, first because you deserved to know, and second because Tommy deserves a father. I would like to think we could work something out together."

"Joint custody?" Miguel's nose wrinkled in distaste.

"Impossible with both of us living in two different countries."

"Not impossible," she countered. "Tommy could visit you in the summer and maybe over the holiday."

"While he lives the rest of the time with you?" Miguel asked. "I hardly think that arrangement is fair."

"Fair? Do you think it was fair to leave me pregnant and alone? I tried to find you, Miguel, but you certainly didn't try to find me. So don't stand there and try to tell me what is or isn't *fair*."

There was a charged silence between them as Kat tried to rein in her temper. She'd long ago accepted that the night she'd spent with Miguel meant nothing to him. Yet deep down she had to admit there was still a small kernel of resentment.

"You're right, Katerina. I must accept responsibility for my actions."

Miguel's acquiescence shocked her. So much that she didn't have any idea how to respond.

"I can only ask that you give me some time now to get to know my son. And, of course, we will need to agree to some financial arrangements."

"I don't want your money, Miguel," she protested. "We're not rich, but we're not poor either."

"I insist," he said. And she could tell by the edge to his tone that there was no point in arguing.

She let out her pent-up breath in a silent sigh. "Fine. We can discuss that more later." She should be thrilled that he hadn't put up much of a fight. But as Miguel left her side to cross over to where Tommy was digging in the dirt with a stick, she couldn't help feeling a sharp stab of disappointment that apparently they wouldn't be raising their son together.

As a family.

Miguel wanted to protest when Katerina insisted it was time to head back to the hotel, but even he could see that Tomas was getting cranky. He didn't doubt her wisdom regarding the fact that their son needed a nap.

He cared for pediatric patients in the hospital, but obviously he didn't know the first thing about raising a child. How was he to know that almost four-year-olds still took naps?

"Up, Mama, up," Tomas whined.

"Is your arm hurting you?" she asked, swinging the boy into her arms and cuddling him close.

Miguel wanted, very badly, to be the one to carry his son, but suspected his offer of assistance wouldn't be welcomed by Tomas. He'd started to make friends with his son, but the boy still clung to his mother for comfort.

"Yeah," Tomas said, burying his face against her neck.

"I'll give you something to make your pain go away when we get back to the hotel room, all right?"

"They gave you pain medication?" he asked in surprise.

"No, but I have children's ibuprofen at the hotel, although I suspect he'll practically be asleep by then, anyway."

Katerina was correct. Tomas had closed his eyes and fully relaxed against his mother by the time they approached the hotel lobby.

"Wait for me here," Katerina told him, as she stabbed

the button to summon the elevator. "I'll only be a few minutes."

He stepped back, resisting the urge to follow her up to their room. He was surprised she'd asked him to wait, figuring she'd want nothing more than to put distance between them. Although it was possible she simply wanted updated information on Juliet.

True to her word, Katerina returned a few minutes later. "Thanks for waiting, Miguel. I'm planning to head over to the hospital, and figured we could ride the metro together."

"I'm happy to ask Fernando to drive us there," he offered.

A grimace flashed over her features, but then she nodded. "I can't get used to the idea of having someone drive me around, but that's fine."

He called Fernando, and then gestured towards a small park bench sitting beneath the trees. "Have a seat. Fernando will be here in a few minutes."

"Why haven't you learned to drive?" she asked.

"I do know how to drive," he said testily, even though, truthfully, it had been a long time since he'd sat behind the wheel. "Fernando is a former patient of mine. He has a wife and three children. He lost his job after his accident and subsequent surgery, so I hired him."

She didn't say anything until Fernando drove up in Miguel's sleek black car. "That was very kind of you, Miguel."

He shrugged and strode forward, opening the back passenger door for her. Once she was seated inside, he closed the door, went around to the other side and slid in.

"Take us to the hospital, please, Fernando," he said in Spanish.

*"Sí, señor,"* Fernando said, his gaze resting curiously on Katerina.

"Juliet is doing better today," he said, as Fernando pulled away from the curb. "Her electrolytes are all within normal range and she's following instructions again. I left orders this morning to begin weaning her off the ventilator."

Katerina smiled and relaxed against the seat. "I'm so happy to hear that. I feel bad I haven't been in there to see her yet today. Sounds as if she'll be ready to return home soon."

Now that he knew Tomas was here in Seville, he wasn't so anxious to pronounce Juliet stable enough for transport back to the U.S., but obviously he couldn't keep Juliet, or Katerina for that matter, hostage here. Maybe he'd be booking that plane ticket to Cambridge after all. "Perhaps," he responded slowly. "But I would like to make sure she's off the ventilator first."

She raised a brow, as if she was able to read his mind. But instead of pushing the issue, she changed the subject. "Tell me, how are DiCarlo and Pedro doing?"

"DiCarlo is still in the I.C.U., but his condition is stable," he admitted. "Pedro is doing well, too. He asked about you this morning. I think he was hurt that you didn't come to visit him."

"I'll visit him this afternoon," she promised. "He's a good kid, Miguel. I know his mother has several other children at home, but it breaks my heart to see him lying in that hospital bed all alone."

"Mine, too, Katerina," he murmured. There was no

denying the soft spot in his heart he had for the boy. "His father is off for weeks at a time as a truck driver, so she isn't ignoring him on purpose. Regardless, I know he'll be thrilled to see you."

The ride to the hospital didn't take long. He put on his lab coat and then gave Fernando some well-deserved time off, seeing as he was close enough to walk home from the hospital.

"I'd like to see Juliet first," Katerina said as they entered the elevator.

"Of course." Several of the staff greeted him as they walked down the hallway of the I.C.U., and if they were surprised to see him once again with Katerina, they didn't say anything to his face. No doubt, there was plenty of gossip going on behind his back and he was glad no one else knew about Tomas.

"Hey, sis, I'm back," Katerina said, as she crossed over to Juliet's bedside. "I'm sorry I couldn't be here earlier, but Tommy was bitten by a dog and I had to bring him to the emergency room."

Miguel was pleasantly surprised when Juliet opened her eyes and turned her face to look at Katerina.

"Juliet! You're awake!" Katerina took her sister's hand and leaned over to press a kiss on her forehead. "I was so worried about you."

Juliet looked as if she wanted to talk, but the breathing tube prevented her from making a sound. Before Miguel could step forward, Katerina took control.

"Don't try to talk—you still have that breathing tube in. But don't worry, Dr. Vasquez is trying to get that removed very soon. Which means you have to cooperate with him. You have to show us that you can breathe okay on your own. Can you understand what I'm saying?"

Juliet nodded and pointed to the tube, demonstrating with hand gestures that she wanted it out.

He crossed over to pick up the clipboard hanging off the end of the bed. "Good afternoon, Juliet. I can see here that your weaning parameters look very good."

Katerina glanced at him, her eyes full of hope. "Does that mean we can get the tube out now?"

He hesitated. Juliet had suffered a seizure just twenty-four hours ago, but he'd been convinced all along that she'd be fine once he got her electrolytes under control. "Let me listen to her lungs first," he said, replacing the clipboard and pulling his stethoscope from the pocket of his lab coat. Katerina went down to crank the head of the bed up so that Juliet was sitting upright. He helped her lean forward so that he could listen to her lung sounds.

"Well?" Katerina demanded when he'd finished.

Even though he knew that this meant Juliet would be discharged back to the U.S. soon, he nodded. "Yes, her lungs sound clear. I will get the nurse to come in and assist."

Katerina looked relieved and stood back as he and Maria, Juliet's nurse, took out her endotracheal tube.

"Water," Juliet croaked.

Katerina quickly came over to hold the small plastic cup and straw up so that Juliet could take a sip.

"Hurts," Juliet whispered hoarsely, putting her hand up to her throat.

"I know. Try to rest," Katerina said, putting a hand

on her arm. "Breathe slow and easy. You're going to be just fine, Jules."

"Where's Mom?" Juliet asked.

Katerina tossed him a worried look. "Mom's gone, Juliet. She passed away three years ago."

"Remember, she's still recovering from her head injury," he murmured.

"Don't talk, Jules. Just relax."

"I thought you were a dream," Juliet said, rubbing her obviously sore throat.

"I'm not a dream. I came as soon as I heard. I love you, Jules. Very much." Bright tears filled Katerina's eyes.

Miguel slipped out of the room, giving the two sisters time to be alone. He was pleased with Juliet's progress, even though he knew she still needed time to recover fully. Yet his heart was heavy as he went back to the nurses' station to write new orders. Obviously, if Juliet continued doing this well, she'd be stable enough to move to a regular room in the morning.

That would give him no choice but to deem her stable enough for transportation back to the U.S. as soon as arrangements could be made.

As he wrote instructions for breathing treatments and another chest X-ray in the morning, he vowed to let his boss know he needed a leave of absence as soon as possible. He couldn't bear the thought of Katerina and Tomas leaving so soon. He'd barely spent an hour with his son. And even though he would consider Katerina's proposed custody arrangements, he wasn't going to give up that easily.

There was no way he was going to settle for some long-distance relationship with Tomas. He was going to need that plane ticket after all.

## CHAPTER TEN

KAT spent several hours with her sister, enormously relieved that she seemed to be doing so much better. But Juliet was also still very confused, not understanding that she was in Spain or that their mother was gone.

When Kat finally left, she was surprised to find Miguel sitting out at the nurses' station, clearly waiting for her. He rose to his feet when he saw her approach.

"Do you have time to visit Pedro?" he asked, meeting her halfway.

She nodded, ashamed to realize she'd completely forgotten about the young teen. "Of course. But you didn't have to stay, Miguel."

"I wanted to," he said simply.

She was touched by his dedication, even though logically she knew that he was glued to her side because of Tommy more than anything. Still, when he put his hand in the small of her back, her traitorous body reacted by shivering with awareness.

When the elevator doors closed, locking the two of them inside, the tension skyrocketed, his familiar scent filling her head. For a moment she couldn't think of anything except the heated kiss they'd shared.

She sneaked a glance at him from beneath her lashes,

wondering if she was losing her mind. Why did she have this strange attraction to him? She'd avoided personal entanglements with men because she didn't want to be left alone, like her mother had been.

Yet here she was, wishing for another chance with Miguel.

The doors opened and she stepped forward quickly, anxious to put space between them.

Thankfully, Pedro was a good distraction, greeting her enthusiastically. "Miss Kat! I'm so glad you came to visit."

"Hi, Pedro," she said, going over to take his hand in hers. She gave him a mock frown. "I hear you're not taking your pain medication as Dr. Vasquez ordered."

"Yes, I am," he corrected. "I took some earlier today when you were here, Dr. Vasquez. Don't you remember?"

Miguel sighed. "Pedro, that was almost eight hours ago. Do you mean to tell me you haven't taken anything since?"

He ducked his head sheepishly. "I wanted to wait until it was nighttime. You said that sleep was important."

Kat put her hands on her hips. "Pedro, you promised me you would take the pain medication."

"I'm sorry. I will take more tonight. Why are you so late here at the hospital?"

"Well, it was quite a busy morning," she said, as Miguel went out into the hall, probably to flag down Pedro's nurse. "I have a four-year-old son named Tommy and he was bitten by a dog so I had to take him to the emergency department to get antibiotics."

"I didn't know you have a son," Pedro said in surprise, and she belatedly realized she hadn't mentioned Tommy earlier. For a moment Pedro seemed almost disappointed by the news, but then he recovered. "Having a dog bite is very scary. Is he okay?"

"He's fine." She refused to look at her watch, not wanting Pedro to think she was in a hurry. Even though she knew Tommy would be up from his nap and ready to eat dinner soon. "But tell me how you're doing, other than not taking your pain medication."

"I walked today, the way Dr. Vasquez told me to. I went up to visit DiCarlo." Pedro grimaced and shrugged. "But I'm bored here with nothing to do all day. One of the nurses did play a word game with me, but she would only use Spanish words. How am I to learn English without practice?"

She'd noticed the game next to his bed. "How about we play a game before I leave? But our rule will be that we only use English words. Okay?"

"Really? You would do that for me?" He looked so happy that she wished she'd thought of it earlier.

"Of course." She pulled out the game and then sat next to his bed. She couldn't just leave, no matter how much she wanted to see Tommy.

"May I join you?" Miguel asked.

"Yes, more players will be more fun," Pedro said excitedly.

As Miguel pulled up a second chair, she realized Miguel would make a wonderful father.

But even as she acknowledged that truth, she knew there was no way to know for sure if he would be just as good a husband.

* * *

At the end of the second game Kat threw up her hands in defeat. "I give up. It's embarrassing to lose to both of you when I'm the one who speaks English."

Miguel flashed a conspiratorial grin at Pedro. "What do you think, amigo? Maybe we should have let her win one."

Pedro nodded. "I think we should have. It's only polite to allow a woman to win."

She rolled her eyes and stood. "I don't need either of you to do me any favors. You each won fair and square. But I'm afraid I need to go. Pedro, I'll visit again tomorrow, okay?"

"Okay. Thank you for staying," Pedro said. "I had much fun."

Miguel also stood. "I'll take you back to the hotel. And, Pedro, take your pain medication, please."

"I will." Pedro looked sad to see them go, but she'd already stayed far longer than she'd planned. She gave him a quick embrace before heading down the hall, anxious to get back to the hotel.

She glanced at Miguel as they waited for the elevator. "I can ride the metro back, there's no reason for you to go out of your way."

He didn't answer until they were inside the elevator. "I would like to see Tommy again, if you wouldn't mind. I thought I would take you all out for dinner."

She wanted to refuse, because being around Miguel was wearying. She was constantly on edge, trying not to let her true feelings show. But glancing up at him and seeing the hope in his eyes, she found she couldn't say no. "Tommy can't wait that late to eat. We usually have dinner at six or six-thirty."

"That's fine with me." When the elevator doors opened on the lobby level, he once again put his hand in the small of her back, gently guiding her. "I will take every moment possible to see my son."

She nodded, realizing with a sense of dread that they would have to make more specific plans for the future, especially now that her sister was doing better. How much longer would Juliet be allowed to stay in Seville? Probably not long. She swallowed hard and tried not to panic.

She wasn't surprised to see that Fernando was waiting outside for them. Now that she knew the reason Miguel had hired him, she found she was happy to have him drive them around. *"Buenos noches,* Fernando," she greeted him.

He flashed a wide smile. *"Buenos noches, señorita."*

"And that's pretty much the extent of my Spanish," she muttered wryly, as she slid into the back seat.

"I'd be happy to teach you," Miguel murmured after he climbed in beside her. "Tomas should learn both languages too."

She bit back a harsh retort, turning to gaze out the window instead. Her anger wasn't entirely rational, yet the last thing she needed was Miguel telling her how to raise her son.

Their son.

Her lack of sleep the night before caught up with her and tears pricked her eyelids. Telling Miguel about Tommy had been the right thing to do so there was no reason to be upset.

"Katerina, what is it? What's wrong?" Miguel asked. He reached over to take her hand and she had to struggle not to yank it away. "Becoming bilingual is a good thing. If my mother hadn't taught me English, I would not have been given the opportunity to study abroad. We never would have met."

And if they hadn't met, Tommy wouldn't exist.

She momentarily closed her eyes, struggling for control. "Miguel, can't you understand how difficult this is for me? Tommy has been my responsibility for almost four years. I was pregnant and alone. I did the best I could. Now it seems like you're planning to barge in and do whatever you want. Without bothering to consult with me."

His hand tightened around her. "Katerina, I am more sorry than you'll ever know about how I left you alone. I will always regret not keeping in touch with you after leaving the U.S. And not just because of the time I missed getting to know my son. But because I realize now how much I missed you."

She sniffed and swiped her free hand over her eyes. "You don't need to flatter me, Miguel. If I hadn't shown up here to visit my sister, we wouldn't have met again. You never would have tried to find me."

There was another long pause. "Katerina, do you believe in fate? Believe that some things just happen for a reason?" His husky voice was low and compelling. "It's true that my dream was to join Doctors Without Borders, and if not for the difficulties with my brother, I probably would not have been here when your sister required emergency care. But I was here. And you arrived with our son. What else could this be if not fate?"

"Coincidence." Even as she said the word, she knew it wasn't entirely true. Was there really some cosmic force at play here? Drawing the two of them together after all this time? She generally believed that hard work and taking responsibility for your choices was the way to get ahead, but she couldn't totally renounce Miguel's beliefs.

"Fate, Katerina," Miguel whispered. "I believe we were meant to be together."

Together? As in as a family? She didn't know what to say to that, and luckily Fernando pulled up in front of her hotel. She gratefully tugged her hand from Miguel's grasp and reached for the doorhandle. "*Gracias,* Fernando," she said, before climbing hastily from the car.

But as quick as she was, Miguel was that much faster. He caught her before she could bolt and gently clasped her shoulders in his large hands. "Katerina, please talk to me. Tell me what has caused you to be so upset?"

She tipped her head back and forced herself to meet his gaze. "I'm more overwhelmed than upset, Miguel. And I'm not sure how you can stand there and claim we were meant to be together. We're not a couple. We're simply two adults who happen to share a child."

One of his hands slid up from her shoulder to cup her cheek. "You can't deny what is between us, *querida.*"

She was about to tell him not to call her darling, but he quickly covered her mouth with his, silencing her with a toe-curling kiss.

She told herself to pull away, even lifted her hands to his chest to push him, but instead her fingers curled in his shirt, yanking him closer as she opened for him, allowing him to deepen the kiss.

All the pent-up emotions she'd tried so hard to ignore came tumbling out in a flash of pure desire. She forgot they were standing on the sidewalk in front of the hotel. Forgot that Fernando was still there, watching them with a huge, satisfied grin.

Forgot that she wasn't going to open herself up to being hurt again.

Everything fell away except this brief moment. A stolen fragment of time when they were able to communicate perfectly without words.

"*Querida,* Katerina, I need you so much," he murmured between steaming-hot kisses. "I can't understand how I lived all this time without you."

She pulled back, gasping for breath, bracing her forehead on his chest, wishing she could believe him. Wishing he'd felt a tenth of what she'd felt for him back then.

"Kat?" the sound of Diana's shocked voice had her jumping away from Miguel.

"Good evening, Diana. Hello, Tommy." Miguel smoothly covered the awkward pause. "Katerina and I were just about to ask you both to join us for dinner."

Kat avoided Diana's accusing gaze as she went over and gathered her son close. "Hi, Tommy, I'm sorry to be gone so long. Are you hungry?"

Tommy nodded. "I'm starving."

"Well, then, let's get going," Miguel said. "I understand there is an American restaurant nearby that serves great food, including hamburgers."

As much as she enjoyed the tangy bite of Spanish food, the thought of a simple American meal was tempting. "We can go somewhere else," she offered.

"Actually, other than smaller places that serve only

*tapas*, the main restaurants don't open this early," Miguel said with a note of apology.

"I'm all in favor of having good old-fashioned hamburgers," Diana said. "But let's hurry, okay? Tommy's bound to get cranky if he doesn't eat soon."

Kat couldn't help feeling guilty all over again. She shouldn't have stayed at the hospital so long. And she really, really shouldn't have kissed Miguel again.

The American restaurant was within walking distance, so Miguel sent Fernando away for a couple of hours. Diana's sour mood evaporated as they enjoyed their meal. When they were finished, Miguel took Tommy over to play a video game, leaving the two women alone.

"Kat, do you think it's smart to get emotionally involved with Miguel?" Diana asked in a low voice.

"I'm already emotionally involved with him, Diana," she responded wearily. "He's Tommy's father, remember? It's not like I can avoid him."

"Avoiding him is very different from having sex with him."

"It was a kiss, Diana." Although she suspected that if they'd been somewhere private, without the added responsibility of caring for Tommy, nothing would have stopped them from making love. "Besides, we'll be going home pretty soon. Juliet woke up and is off the breathing machine. She's still confused, but she's doing a lot better. I'm certain she'll be stable enough to be transferred home very soon."

"Already?" Diana looked disappointed with the news. "But we've hardly had time to sightsee."

"I know. I'm sorry." She did feel bad that Diana had

been stuck babysitting Tommy. "Maybe tomorrow I can take Tommy to the hospital to visit Juliet, giving you time to go see the cathedral. I hear it's spectacular."

"All right. But what about Miguel? What's he going to do?"

Good question. "I'm not sure, but I suspect he'll come visit me and Tommy in Cambridge. After that, I just don't know."

Diana was silent for a moment. "Are you going to move to Seville?"

"No!" Kat stared at her friend in shock. "Of course not. What on earth gave you that idea?"

Before Diana could respond, Miguel and Tommy returned to the table. "We blowed things up," Tommy said excitedly. "Bang, bang, bang!"

Kat grimaced and glanced at Miguel, who didn't look the least bit repentant. "Tommy has very good hand-eye coordination," he said proudly. "We scored many points."

They left the restaurant a little while later so that Miguel could enjoy this time with his son. They went for a long walk, enjoying the warm night air.

When they returned to the hotel, Tommy was definitely looking tired. "I'll take him upstairs, he'll need a bath before bed," Diana said.

Kat enjoyed giving Tommy his bath, but before she could utter a protest, Miguel spoke up. "Thank you, Diana. I have a few things to discuss with Katerina."

"No problem," Diana said with false brightness. "Say goodnight to your mom, Tommy."

"G'night." Tommy held out his chubby arms for a

hug and a kiss. And then he shocked her by reaching over to give Miguel a hug and a kiss too.

"Goodnight, Tomas," Miguel murmured, as he finally set Tommy down on the sidewalk.

They stood for several moments until Diana and Tommy had gone into the elevator of the hotel. Kat rubbed her hands over her arms, suddenly chilled in her short-sleeved blouse and Capri pants, uncertain what exactly Miguel wanted to talk about.

"Katerina, would you join me for a drink?" Miguel asked, as Fernando pulled up.

A drink? Or something more? The kiss they'd shared simmered between them and suddenly she knew he planned to pick up where they'd left off before Diana had interrupted them.

"Please?" He reached over to take her hand in his.

She hesitated, feeling much like she had four and a half years ago when Miguel had asked her out after losing their young patient. But she was older now, and wiser. She shouldn't be a victim to her hormones.

When he lifted her hand and pressed a kiss to the center of her palm, her good intentions flew away.

"Yes, Miguel," she murmured. "I'd love to."

# CHAPTER ELEVEN

MIGUEL could barely hide the surge of satisfaction when Katerina agreed to have a drink with him. He took her hand and turned to head outside where Fernando was waiting inside the car parked out at the curb.

"Where are we going?" she asked, when they stepped outside into the warm night air.

"My place will provide us with the most privacy," he murmured, gently steering her towards the car. When she stiffened against him, disappointment stabbed deep. "Unless you'd rather go somewhere else?"

He practically held his breath as she hesitated. Finally she shook her head and prepared to climb into the back seat of the car. "No, that's okay. Your place is fine," she agreed.

His relief was nearly overwhelming, and as he rounded the car to climb in beside her, it took every ounce of willpower he possessed not to instruct Fernando to break the speed limit to get to his apartment as soon as possible. Once he was seated beside her, he reached over and took her hand. "I want you to know, Katerina, I think you have done an amazing job with raising our son."

She glanced at him in surprise. "For some reason, I keep expecting you to be angry with me."

No, he was only angry with himself. "After tonight it is easier for me to understand your desire to protect Tomas from being hurt." He'd been surprised at the strong surge of protectiveness he'd felt when he'd spent time with his son this evening. "But I hope you can also trust me enough to know I would never willingly do anything to upset him."

"I do trust you, Miguel." Her soft admission caused the tension to seep from his shoulders, allowing him to relax against the buttery-soft leather seats. "Somehow we'll find a way to work this out."

He wanted to do more than to just work things out, but he refrained from saying anything that might cause an argument, unwilling to risk ruining their fragile truce. He wanted this time they had together to be special. So he kept her hand in his, brushing his thumb across the silky smoothness of her skin.

Katerina was always beautiful to him, no matter what she wore. Even dressed casually, in a short-sleeved green blouse that matched her eyes and a pair of black knee-length leggings that displayed her shapely legs, she was breathtaking.

Fernando pulled up in front of his apartment and he reluctantly let her go in order to open the door to climb out. She didn't say anything as they made their way up to his apartment. Once inside, he crossed over to the small kitchen. "What would you like to drink?" he asked.

"Um, a glass of red wine would be nice," she said, clutching her hands together as if nervous.

"Excellent choice." He pulled out a bottle of his favorite Argentinean wine from the rack and quickly removed the cork before pouring them two glasses. She stood awkwardly in the center of the living room as he approached and handed her the glass.

"I feel like I should make a toast," he murmured as he handed her one glass and tipped his so that the rims touched. "To the most beautiful mother in the world."

She blushed and rolled her eyes, taking a step backwards. "Exaggerate much?" she asked, her tone carrying an edge.

He wasn't exaggerating at all, but he could see she was struggling to hold him at arm's length, as if uncomfortable with drawing attention to herself. Or believing in herself.

That thought brought him up short, and he paused, wondering if his leaving so abruptly after their magical night together had caused her to lose some of her self-confidence.

If so, he'd wronged her in more ways than one.

"Katerina, why do you doubt my feelings?" he asked softly. "Surely my attraction to you is no secret by now. Four and a half years ago I succumbed to the keen awareness between us. And obviously that same attraction hasn't faded over time."

"But you still left," she pointed out.

"Yes, but if my father hadn't suffered his stroke, I'm sure that we would have continued to see each other." He knew that he wouldn't have possessed the strength to stay away. Even for her sake.

She eyed him over the rim of her wineglass. "You don't know that, Miguel. Rumor amongst the O.R. staff

was that you didn't want any emotional attachments because you weren't planning to stay in the U.S. I doubt
that you would have changed your mind about that,
even for me."

He shouldn't have been surprised to know his plans
had been fodder for gossip, but he was. There had been
many women who'd expressed interest in him, and he'd
often used that line to avoid entanglements. "I can't
deny that I wasn't planning to stay. I didn't keep my
dream of joining Doctors Without Borders a secret.
And even then I was hesitant to start a relationship
with an American."

She looked shocked by his revelation. "Why?"

He wished he hadn't gone down this path. "My
mother was American and she wasn't happy living here
in Spain. But that part isn't important now. Suffice it to
say that had I stayed three more months to finish my
trauma surgery fellowship, I would have been there
when you discovered you were pregnant. If not for my
father's stroke, we could have handled things very differently." He wasn't sure exactly how, but at least he
would have known about his son.

She stared at him for several long moments. "Maybe.
But playing the what-if game isn't going to help. We
can't go back and change the past."

"I don't want to change the past, Katerina," he countered. "I wouldn't give up Tomas for anything. Yet this
evening isn't about our son. It is about you and me."

Her lips parted in shock, making a small O, and she
carefully set down her wineglass as if afraid she might
drop it. "I don't understand."

Obviously he wasn't being very articulate. "Perhaps you would allow me to show you what I mean instead."

When she didn't voice an objection, he stepped closer and drew her deliberately into his arms. He didn't pounce but stared deep into her eyes so that she could read his intent and see the desire he felt for her. When she still didn't utter a protest, he lowered his mouth to capture hers.

She held herself stiffly in his arms, and just when he thought she would push him away, she softened against him and opened her mouth, welcoming his kiss.

Desire thundered in his chest and he gathered her closer still, pulling her softness firmly against his hard muscles and tipping her head back so that he could explore her mouth more fully.

He forced himself to take his time, savoring the exotic taste, when all he really wanted to do was to rip their clothing out of the way so that he could explore every inch of her skin.

"Miguel," she gasped, when he finally freed her mouth in order to explore the sexy curve of her jaw, the hollow behind her ear.

"Say yes, Katerina," he murmured between kisses. He wanted to make love to her, right here, right now. "Say yes."

He continued his leisurely exploration, kissing his way down her neck, dipping further to the enticing valley between her breasts, as if waiting for her answer wasn't killing him.

"Yes, Miguel," she whispered in a ragged voice, arching her back to give him better access to her breasts. "Yes!"

He didn't trust his voice so he swept Katerina up into his arms and strode down the hall to his bedroom, hoping and praying that she wouldn't change her mind.

Kat didn't allow herself to second-guess her decision, every nerve-ending was on fire for Miguel. She hadn't felt this way since their one and only night together. No other man made her feel as beautiful and desirable as Miguel did.

When he swept her into his arms, she pressed her mouth against the hollow in his neck, nipping and licking, savoring his scent and enjoying the way his arms tightened around her in response.

In his bedroom he flipped on a single lamp and then paused near the bed. He gently slid her body down the front of his so that she could feel the full extent of his desire. She shivered, but not with cold, when he unbuttoned her blouse and shoved the cotton fabric aside, revealing her sheer green bra and then ultimately the matching sheer green panties.

She was grateful she'd worn decent underwear, even though it didn't stay on long. She should have felt self-conscious to be naked before him, but she wasn't. His gaze devoured her as he quickly stripped off his own clothes.

"Katerina, *mi amore*," he muttered as he gently placed her on his bed, before covering her body with his. "I don't deserve you."

She was pretty sure he had that backwards, but then she wasn't thinking at all because he'd lowered his mouth to the tip of her breast. She writhed impatiently beneath him but he took his time, giving equal attention to both breasts before trailing kisses down her abdomen to her belly button. And then lower still.

There was a brief moment when she worried about the faint stretch marks along her lower abdomen, but when he swept long kisses over every single one, the last vestiges of doubt vanished. She was practically sobbing with need when he finally spread her legs and probed deep, making sure she was ready.

"Now, Miguel," she rasped.

His dark eyes glittered with desire but he simply shook his head and dipped his head again, this time replacing his fingers with his tongue. Something he'd done that first time they'd made love.

Her orgasm hit fast and hard, deep shudders racking her body. He quickly rose up, rolled a condom on with one hand before he thrust deep, causing yet another orgasm to roll over her.

She was sure she couldn't take much more, but he whispered to her in Spanish, lifting her hips so they fit more snugly together, gently encouraging her to match his rhythm. Slow and deep at first, and then faster and faster, until they simultaneously soared up and over the peak of pleasure.

Kat couldn't move and not just because of Miguel's body sprawled across hers. Every muscle in her body had the consistency of jelly, making it impossible to move even if she wanted to.

Which she didn't.

After several long moments Miguel lifted himself up and rolled over, bringing her along with him, so that she was now lying fully against him. She rested her head against his chest, listening to the rapid beat of his heart.

The chirping sound of a cellphone broke the silence and she froze, trying to remember if that was how her small disposable cellphone sounded. Was Diana calling because Tommy needed her? Maybe the dog bite on his arm was getting infected?

When Miguel muttered something in Spanish beneath his breath, she realized the call wasn't for her. It was for him. There was a strong sense of déjà vu as she remembered the phone call he'd received the morning after the night they'd spent together. She forced herself to lift her head, to look at him. "Do you need to get that? Is that the hospital?"

"I'm not on call tonight," he said with a dark scowl. "Whoever it is can wait."

After several rings the phone went silent and she relaxed against him. When she shivered, he pulled up the sheet and blanket to cover her. She would have been happy to stay like this with him for the rest of the night, but she knew she should go back to the hotel in case Tommy needed her.

She couldn't help thinking about what he'd revealed earlier about his mother being American and not liking it here in Spain. She'd known his mother had spoken fluent English, which had been how he'd picked up the language so quickly.

But what did this all mean about the future?

A loud buzzer sounded, echoing loudly across the apartment, startling her. Miguel muttered something rude before pulling away from her.

He fumbled for his clothing, pulling on his pants be-

fore heading out to answer the door. She was grateful
he closed the bedroom door, giving her privacy.

She didn't hesitate but quickly found her clothes and
got dressed, hardly able to contain her curiosity about
who'd come to Miguel's home at ten o'clock at night.
She crossed the room, trying to listen, unsure if she
should go out there or not. When she heard a female
voice speaking in rapid Spanish she froze, the blood
draining from her face.

Was it possible that Miguel was actually involved
with a woman after all?

Miguel wasn't the least bit happy to see the woman
his brother used to date standing on the other side of
the door. He tried to rein in his temper. "What do you
want, Corrina?"

"Luis is missing, Miguel. I need you to help me find
him."

Corrina was a pretty girl with dark wavy hair, who
for some unknown, self-destructive reason was still
hung up on his brother, despite the fact that Luis had
broken her heart more than once.

"Come in," he said rather ungraciously, stepping
back to give her room to enter. "How do you know
he's missing?"

"He spent last night at my place but this morning he
was gone. I've looked everywhere for him, Miguel. He's
not at home or working on the olive farm or at any of
his usual hang-outs." Corrina's eyes filled with tears.
"I'm afraid something has happened to him."

He suppressed a sigh. His brother wasn't exactly
known for his tact and could very easily have been

looking for an excuse to avoid Corrina. "Did you no-
tify the police?"

"Yes, but they said there's nothing they can do."
Corrina stared up at him defiantly. "I know everyone
thinks he's avoiding me, but I don't think so. Something
is wrong, Miguel. I feel it here," she said, dramatically
putting her hand over her heart.

The concern in her eyes was real enough, but he
didn't share her fears. Besides, he didn't want to end
things so abruptly with Katerina. Not again. Not when
their time here in Seville was so limited.

But then his bedroom door opened and Katerina
emerged, fully dressed, and with a sinking heart
he knew their evening had already come to an end.
"Excuse me, I was just leaving," she said, avoiding his
gaze as she swung her purse over her shoulder and
headed for the door.

"Katerina, wait. This is Corrina Flores, my brother's girlfriend. It seems she believes Luis is missing."

There was a flash of surprise on Katerina's face and
she paused, glancing back with concern. He realized
she'd assumed the worst, believing Corrina was one
of his former lovers. He was frustrated by her lack of
trust yet at the same time grimly pleased that she cared
enough to be jealous.

"Missing since when?" Katerina asked.

"Just since this morning. I'm sure he's fine, there's
no need to rush off." Selfishly, he wanted her to stay,
needed her support as he looked for his brother.

She grimaced and toyed with the strap of her purse.
"Actually, I really should go, Miguel. I want to be there

in case Tommy wakes up. The dog bite may cause him some pain."

He understood, even though he didn't want to let her go. There was so much yet that they needed to discuss before he released Juliet to return home. He'd used the short time they'd had together to make love, rather than planning their future.

Something he couldn't quite bring himself to regret.

"All right, let me call Fernando, he'll drive you back to the hotel. Why don't we plan to get together first thing in the morning? I'll take you and Tommy out for breakfast and then we'll visit your sister."

"Ah, sure. But don't bother Fernando this late," she protested. "I'll take the metro."

"It's no bother. He's probably just finishing dinner and I'll need his assistance myself, anyway." He certainly wouldn't allow her to go back to the hotel alone. And as much as he wanted to spend more time with Katerina, he couldn't bring himself to ignore Corrina's concerns about Luis.

"I hope you find your brother," Katerina murmured.

"I'm sure we will. And it's about time he learns to take responsibility for his actions. Luis can't expect me to keep bailing him out." He didn't bother to hide his annoyance.

Corrina wisely kept silent as he called Fernando and then walked Katerina outside.

"Thank you, Katerina, for an evening I'll never forget," he whispered, hugging her close and giving her another heated kiss.

"Goodnight, Miguel," she murmured, breaking away from his embrace and climbing into the back seat of the car. He couldn't help feeling as if he'd said something wrong when she ignored him to chat with Fernando.

Grinding his teeth together, he had little choice but to shut the car door and step back, allowing Fernando to drive Katerina away. He stared after the red tail-lights, fighting the urge to demand Fernando return at once so he could figure out what had caused Katerina to be upset.

Annoyed with himself, and his brother, he reluctantly turned and went back upstairs to where Corrina waited. All he could think was that he'd better not find out that his brother was simply trying to avoid his old girlfriend or he wouldn't hesitate to box Luis's ears.

This was the second time his family problems had pulled him away from Katerina. And he was determined that it would also be the last.

# CHAPTER TWELVE

THE following morning, Kat was surprised when Miguel didn't show up as promised. As Tommy was hungry, she and Diana took him out for breakfast. As they enjoyed fresh pastries, she couldn't help wondering if Miguel had found his brother or if he'd stayed up the entire night, searching for him.

"I'll take Tommy with me to see Juliet now that she's doing better," she offered. "That way you can go and see the cathedral before we have to leave."

"If you're sure you don't mind," Diana said, before shoving the last bit of pastry in her mouth.

"I don't mind at all." In truth she would have loved to see the cathedral too, but coming to Seville hadn't been a vacation for her. She'd only come because her sister had been injured.

And there was a strong possibility she'd be back in the not-too-distant future if Tommy was going to be spending time with his father. She glanced around, silently admitting that, as beautiful as Seville was, she couldn't really imagine living here.

Once again she found herself thinking about Miguel's mother. Clearly he'd avoided dating anyone back in the

U.S. because he didn't plan to relocate to the U.S. on a permanent basis.

And considering the problems he'd had with his brother, she couldn't imagine him changing his mind. Which left them where? Back to a joint custody but separate countries type of arrangement?

She would have been satisfied with that before, but not any more. Not since making love with Miguel. She wanted it all.

She wanted a true family.

"Mama, go. Now," Tommy said insistently.

"Okay, I'm ready." She paid the bill and then used a wet napkin to clean up Tommy's sticky fingers. "We're going to go visit Aunt Juliet. Won't that be fun?"

He nodded vigorously and dropped from the chair, making her grin at the amount of energy radiating off his tiny frame. Had Miguel been the same way as a child? She suspected he had been.

She started walking toward the nearest metro stop, holding Tommy's hand as they took the stairs down to the lower level. There was a strong possibility that if Miguel had gotten home late, he'd decided to simply meet her at the hospital.

Suspecting that her sister might have already been moved out of the I.C.U., she stopped at the front desk. *"¿Donde esta mi hermana*, Juliet Campbell?" Where is my sister?

There was a flood of Spanish that she didn't understand. When she looked blankly at the woman, she wrote down the room number and handed it to Kat.

*"Gracias,"* she murmured, looking down at Juliet's

new room number, 202. "This way, Tommy," she said, steering him toward the elevator.

Juliet was sitting up at the side of the bed, finishing her breakfast, when they entered. Kat was very relieved to find her sister looking much better. She crossed the room to give Juliet a hug. "Hey, sis, how are you feeling today?"

"Kat! You brought Tommy, too?"

"Yes. Tommy, you remember Aunt Juliet, right? Can you say hi to her?"

"Hi," Tommy said, and then ducked his head, refusing to relinquish Kat's hand.

"Hi, Tommy. It's good to see you. Wanna see my cast?" Juliet said, moving the blankets off her right leg.

Ever curious, the cast was enough to draw Tommy forward. He knelt beside Juliet's right leg, lifting his fist to knock on the fiberglass cast.

"Don't worry, that's the one part of my body that doesn't hurt," Juliet muttered dryly.

"Are you in pain, Jules?" she asked, moving closer. "Dr. Vasquez told me that you had some cracked ribs, too."

"Everything hurts," her sister admitted. "And don't bother asking me what happened, I honestly can't remember."

"Don't worry, I'm sure your memory will return in time." Although there was certainly no guarantee. The numerous bruises and lacerations were already starting to fade, but Kat could well imagine that her sister's muscles were also still sore.

She wanted to ask her sister more questions, to make

sure Juliet wasn't as confused as she had been yesterday, but they were interrupted by a knock at the door.

"Good morning, Juliet," a plump woman greeted her
sister. "And you must be Katerina Richardson. Nice to
meet you in person."

Kat stared at the woman, certain she hadn't met her
before. She would have remembered someone speaking
English, for one thing. The familiarity of the stranger's
greeting was unnerving.

"My name is Susan Horton and I'm the study abroad
program coordinator. I'm the one who contacted you
about Juliet's accident, remember?"

Of course she remembered now. So much had happened since the first day she'd arrived, she'd completely
forgotten about the woman. "Yes."

"I'm glad you're both here," Susan said, "because
we need to make immediate arrangements for Juliet's
transfer back to the United States."

Kat tried to hide her shock. "So soon? Don't we need
Dr. Vasquez to sign off on Juliet's case first?"

"There's another doctor covering for Dr. Vasquez
today, and he's already given his approval. So, if you'd
come with me, we'll begin making the necessary arrangements."

"Right now?" Kat cast a helpless glance toward her
sister, before following Susan out of the room. She could
only hope Miguel would show up soon or they might
have to leave without saying goodbye.

Miguel shouldn't have been surprised to find Luis in
jail. His friend, Rafael Hernandez, had finally called
him to let him know Luis had been driving under the

influence. He'd called Corrina to make sure she knew, but then he debated with himself over whether or not to post Luis's bond. It wasn't the money but the principle of bailing his brother out of trouble again.

In the end they wouldn't let him post bail until the morning. Which ruined his plans to meet Katerina and Tomas for breakfast.

"Thanks for picking me up," Luis said, wincing at the bright light.

"Luis, you're either going to kill yourself or someone else if you don't stop this," Miguel said with a heavy sigh. "You'd better figure out what you want to do with the rest of your life, and quick."

"Don't worry about me, just go on your stupid mission trip," his brother muttered, scrubbing his hand over his jaw.

"I'm not going to Africa, I'm going back to the U.S., at least temporarily." He glanced over to where Luis was slouched in the corner of the car. "I have a son, Luis. A son I didn't know about until just a few days ago. But he and his mother live in Cambridge, Massachusetts."

Luis lifted his head and peered at him with bloodshot eyes. "You're going to live there? With them?"

He hadn't realized until just now how much he wanted to be with Katerina and Tomas on a full-time basis, but he wasn't keen on living in the U.S. for ever. Yet he couldn't ask Katerina to move here, not when she had her sister to worry about. And even once Juliet was better, he didn't want to risk the same thing happening to Katerina that had happened to his mother. He couldn't wait to see Katerina and talk to her about his idea of moving to the U.S. temporarily.

"I'm not sure where I want to live, but I do want to be a part of my son's life," he said slowly. "But I can't leave you like this, Luis. You need help. Professional help."

His brother was silent for a long moment. "Will you let me sell the olive farm?" he asked.

Shocked by the question, Miguel nearly swerved into the other lane. "You want to sell the farm? Why? What will you do to support yourself?"

"I've always wanted to work in construction," Luis admitted. "I hate farming. I want to build things. Houses, buildings."

Build things? He turned to stare at his brother, stunned by his revelation. Granted, Luis had built a new warehouse on the farm last year, but all this time he'd had no clue that his brother hated farming.

"Are you sure about this, Luis?" he asked. "Once you sell the farm, there's no going back."

"I'm sure. Corrina's father wants me to help in his construction company. I've been trying to get up the nerve to ask you about selling the farm."

"Do you think working for her father is wise? You haven't treated Corrina very well these past few years."

"I know I've made a mess of my life," Luis said in a low voice. "But I really want to do this, Miguel. I know the farm has been in our family for generations, but I feel trapped there. It's too far from town, for one thing. I realized when I built the new warehouse that I gained more satisfaction from doing that than all the years I've spent picking olives. And I care about Corrina. I kept breaking things off because I couldn't imagine raising a family on the farm. I keep remembering how Mom died there."

He couldn't hide his surprise yet at the same time he understood how Luis felt. "Why didn't you say something sooner?" he asked.

"I was afraid you would be upset. You and Papa always talked about how the Vasquez farm had sustained families for generations. That it was a family tradition."

Miguel winced, knowing Luis was right. He hadn't stayed on the farm, choosing to go into medicine at the university as soon as he'd been able to. It shamed him to realize he hadn't ever asked Luis what he wanted to do. "I'm sorry, Luis. I never realized how badly you wanted to leave the farm, too."

"So you're not mad?" Luis asked, looking pathetically eager despite his rough night in a jail cell. "Because Señor Guadalupe once asked me about selling. I would like to call him to see if he's still interested. If he will buy the farm, I can start working for Corrina's father right away."

"I'm not mad, Luis," he said. "By all means, call Señor Guadalupe. If he's not interested, let me know. I'll see what I can do to help."

Fernando pulled into the driveway of the Vasquez olive farm, and for a moment Miguel simply sat there, staring out at the rows upon rows of olive trees.

It was a little sad to think of selling the farm to strangers, yet at the same time he was a doctor. A surgeon. Saving lives was important and satisfying. He'd never planned on working the farm himself, yet had he subconsciously forced Luis into the role because he hadn't wanted to let go of the past?

The idea was humbling.

"Thanks for the ride," Luis said as he climbed from the car.

"Let me know when you have a buyer lined up."

"I will." Luis looked positively happy and waved as Fernando backed out of the driveway. He then headed into the house.

"Are you really moving to the U.S.?" Fernando asked from the front seat.

He met the older man's gaze in the rear-view mirror. "Yes, for a while, Fernando."

Fernando nodded. "Señor Vasquez, I wonder if you would be so kind as to give me a reference before you go so that I can apply for a job."

Miguel mentally smacked himself in the forehead. Why hadn't he thought of this earlier? "Fernando, how do you feel about being an olive farmer?"

"I would be willing to learn."

He grinned and reached for his cellphone. Everything was going to work out just fine. Luis didn't need to bother Señor Guadalupe after all.

Fate had helped him out once again.

Kat could only sit in stunned silence as Susan Horton finalized her sister's travel arrangements. Everything was set. They would be leaving Seville by one-thirty that afternoon. It was the latest flight out, and they wouldn't arrive back in the U.S. until nearly ten o'clock at night, but when Kat had tried to protest, Susan had remained firm that Juliet would be on that flight, regardless of whether or not Kat wanted to go with her. Given that choice, she'd quickly arranged for additional seating for herself, Diana and Tommy.

She'd also called Diana right away, arranging to meet back at the hotel immediately. The airport was only thirty minutes away, but they would need to get there by eleven-thirty, two hours before departure time, and it was already almost ten now. They had just over an hour to get back to the hotel, pack and check out of the hotel.

She left the hospital, carrying Tommy to make better time. Luckily the metro ran often and it didn't take her long to get to the hotel. She didn't waste any time tossing stuff into their suitcases.

"I can't believe they're making us leave today," Diana said as she helped Kat pack Tommy's things. "Like letting your sister stay one more day would make such a big difference?"

"I know. Although I suspect if they had come to visit Juliet on Sunday, they would have made us leave on an earlier flight."

"I suppose. Okay, that's everything," Diana said. They'd worked like speed demons, and had managed to get everything together in twenty-minutes flat.

Kat made one more sweep of the room, making sure Tommy hadn't left anything behind. "All right, let's haul all this down to the lobby so we can check out."

"What about Miguel?" Diana asked, as they crowded into the elevator.

"As stupid as it sounds, I don't have his phone number." Miguel was on Kat's mind, especially after the night they'd shared, and because they still hadn't made plans for the future. Kat had hoped that Miguel would show up at the hospital before they left, but she hadn't seen him. And now they'd be leaving the hotel shortly. "I'm sure he'll figure out what happened once he dis-

covers Juliet has been discharged." She wished she
didn't have to leave without saying goodbye, though.

"Did you guys decide on some sort of joint custody
arrangement?" Diana asked.

"I'm not sure if we really agreed on that or not," she
said truthfully. She hadn't told Diana about the evening
she'd spent making love with Miguel either. Had she
done the right thing by saying yes to Miguel? If only
she'd waited. Obviously, it would have been smarter of
her to avoid getting emotionally involved. Again.

"Stay here with Tommy while I check out." Kat
crossed over to the counter, asking for the bill and for
a taxi to take them to the airport where they would
meet up with Juliet.

They arrived at the small Seville airport with time to
spare, so they stopped for something to eat. Kat could
barely concentrate—she kept scanning the area, looking for any sign of Miguel.

Where was he? Surely once he'd gone to the hospital and realized Juliet had been discharged, he would
know to come and find her at the airport. Something
bad must have happened to Luis for him to not be here.

Unless he'd changed his mind about being a part of
Tommy's life?

No, she couldn't believe that. Not after the way he'd
made love to her. Not after everything they'd shared.

Although she couldn't help coming back to the fact
that he'd never wanted to be with an American. Like her.

"Kat, look, there's your sister."

She looked over in time to see Susan Horton pushing Juliet in a wheelchair through the small terminal,
followed by an airport employee wheeling Juliet's large

suitcase. "Watch Tommy for a minute, okay?" Kat said, before hurrying over to her sister.

"Hey, Jules, how are you?" Kat tried not to be upset at the way they were being rushed out of there. "Are you in pain?"

"I have her pain medication right here," Susan said before Juliet could answer. The woman's brisk, impersonal attitude made Kat grind her teeth in frustration. "Now, is there anything else you need? If not, I'll be leaving Juliet in your hands."

Kat wrestled her temper under control. "We'll be fine," she said, taking over the task of pushing Juliet's wheelchair.

"Are you ready to go through security?" Diana asked, holding onto Tommy's hand. They needed the assistance of two airport employees to manage their luggage.

She sighed, glancing back over the crowd of people one more time, wishing more than anything that Miguel would come. But there was still no sign of him. As much as she wanted to wait, getting Juliet and Tommy through the airport security line would be difficult and time-consuming. She didn't dare wait much longer.

"Sure thing. Let's go."

Going through security took far longer than she could have imagined, especially with Juliet needing so much assistance. She tried not to think about the fact that they would have to change planes four times, before arriving at home. Once they were finished with security, they put their carry-on luggage back together and made their way down to their assigned gate.

Diana flopped into one of the hard plastic chairs with

a groan. "Somehow, going home isn't nearly as much fun," she muttered.

Kat pasted a smile on her face, unwilling to let on how much she was hurting inside, as she made sure Juliet was comfortable.

She'd really, really, expected Miguel to show up here at the airport. And now that he hadn't—she wasn't sure what to think.

Had he changed his mind about wanting to be a father to Tommy? Did he regret making love to her? She wished she knew more about Miguel's mother. He'd mentioned she'd died several years ago, when he'd still been in high school. Whatever had happened had made him determined not to become emotionally involved with an American.

With her.

Her heart squeezed with pain and tears pricked her eyes as she realized she'd foolishly fallen in love with Miguel.

## CHAPTER THIRTEEN

MIGUEL strode into the hospital, knowing he was beyond late. He wasn't due to work today but he knew Katerina would come to visit her sister.

He walked into room 202 and stopped abruptly when he saw an elderly man lying in the bed. He frowned and glanced at the room number, making sure he had the correct one.

After murmuring a quick apology, he spun around and went back to the nurses' station. They must have moved Juliet to a different room for some unknown reason.

But, no, her name wasn't on the board at all. With a frown he picked up the phone, intending to call down to the front desk, when he saw his colleague, Felipe. "Felipe, where's my patient, Juliet Campbell?" he asked.

Felipe turned around. "Miguel, what are you doing here? I thought I was to cover your patients today?"

"You are, but I was actually looking for Juliet's sister, Katerina. What room did Juliet get moved to?"

Felipe looked puzzled. "I discharged her, Miguel. Señora Horton from the study abroad program wanted her to be sent back to the U.S., so I went ahead and gave the discharge order."

"What?" A knot of dread formed in his gut and he grew angry with himself for not anticipating that something like this might happen. He'd known the minute he'd given the orders to have Juliet transferred to a regular room that her time here was limited. "When? How long ago?"

Felipe shrugged. "I'm not sure, maybe two or three hours?"

Three hours? No! He struggled to remain calm as he glanced at the clock. It was almost eleven-thirty already. "Was that when you wrote the order? Or when she actually left?"

"I didn't pay attention," Felipe admitted. "Miguel, what's the problem? Clearly, she was stable enough to travel."

He forced a smile, knowing none of this was Felipe's fault. "I trust your judgment. Excuse me but I need to catch up with them." Before Felipe could say anything more, he left, lengthening his stride to hurry as he called Fernando, instructing his driver to meet him outside.

"We need to stop at home, so I can get my passport. From there we're heading straight to the airport," he said, the moment he slid into the back seat. A few days ago, when he'd reviewed flights out of Seville heading to the U.S., he'd noticed the last flight was at one o'clock in the afternoon.

He grabbed his passport, and not much else. He'd have to buy what he needed once he arrived in the U.S. Back in the car, he called the airline in an attempt to book a seat as Fernando navigated the city streets.

"I'm sorry, but we can't book any more seats at this

time," the woman said. "We stop selling tickets two hours before the flight."

He resisted the urge to smack his fist on the counter. "I need to get on that flight. I'm sure you can make an exception."

There was a pause, and he held his breath. "I'll check with my supervisor," she finally said.

He tightened his grip on the phone, willing Fernando to hurry. But the traffic was heavy today, and they were moving at a snail's pace. The airport was normally a thirty-minute drive, and he could only hope and pray that the traffic would break soon. He had to get there in time. He had to!

"I'm sorry, Señor Vasquez. We are not able to sell you a ticket."

He closed his eyes and swallowed a curse. He forced himself to be polite. "Thank you for checking."

"Problems?" Fernando asked, catching his gaze in the rear-view mirror.

He shook his head. "Just get to the airport as soon as possible. I want to see Katerina before she leaves."

He'd have to buy a ticket in order to get past security, but at this point he was willing to do anything to see Katerina, talk to her one more time before she and Tommy boarded that plane. The panic that gripped him by the throat surprised him. He hadn't realized until she was gone just how much he cared about Katerina.

It wasn't just that he missed his son. Katerina would agree to share custody, he knew. But at this moment he didn't care about custody arrangements.

He cared about Katerina.

* * *

When the airline attendant asked for all passengers needing help to board, Katerina stood up. "I think that means us. Are you ready to go, Juliet?"

"Sure." Her sister already looked exhausted and they hadn't even started their long flight. Kat couldn't suppress a flash of anger toward Susan Horton for rushing Juliet out so fast. As Diana had said earlier, what was one more day?

Maybe she should have put up more of a fight, even though Susan Horton hadn't been interested in listening to reason. Besides, it was too late now. She bent over to release the locks on the wheelchair and then pushed her sister forward, leaving Diana and Tommy to follow.

Getting Juliet safely transferred into an aisle seat was no easy task. The only good thing was that they were given a spot in the front row of a section, leaving plenty of room for her leg that was still in a cast. Juliet groaned under her breath as she used the crutches, favoring her right side where she had her cracked ribs.

They were both sweating by the time they were finally settled. Diana and Tommy were immediately behind them, which was a mixed blessing.

"Tommy, stop kicking the seat," she said for the third time, trying not to snap at him. "It feels like you're kicking me in the back."

"Sorry, Mama."

"Do you want me to switch places with him?" Diana asked, leaning forward anxiously as if sensing her frayed nerves.

"No, he'll only end up kicking Juliet." She was tense and crabby but did her best not to let it show as her bad mood certainly wasn't Tommy's fault. Or Diana's. Or Juliet's.

She was upset because she'd really expected Miguel to come to the airport to find her. But for all she knew, he was still looking for his brother. She tried to tell herself that this way was for the better. Things had moved pretty fast between she and Miguel so a little time and distance would likely be good for both of them.

Yet regret at leaving Seville so abruptly filled her chest, squeezing her lungs. There hadn't been time to say goodbye to Pedro. As the plane slowly filled up with passengers, she wondered how Miguel would manage to find her in Cambridge.

If he decided to come at all.

Miguel purchased a ticket to Madrid and managed to get through security in time to find Katerina's plane had just started to board. He rushed over to the gate and swept his gaze over the group of passengers. After several long moments he was forced to admit they must have already boarded. Which made sense, as Juliet had a broken leg and had probably needed help to get into her seat.

He went up to the desk. "Excuse me, but I need to speak to passenger, Katerina Richardson. I think she may already be on the plane."

"I'm sorry, but there's nothing I can do. You're not allowed on the plane without a boarding pass," the attendant said with a false smile.

So close. He was so close! "Just five minutes. You could ask her to come back out here and I promise she'll be back on the plane in five minutes."

"I'm sorry, Señor, I can't help you." The woman's false smile faded and he could see a security guard making his way over. She glanced past him as if he weren't there. "May I help you?" she asked the next person in line.

Miguel quickly left the counter, preferring to avoid the security guard. He still had a ticket to Madrid, and from there he was sure there would be a better selection of flights to the U.S. But considering his flight didn't leave for two more hours, he knew there was no chance in the world of arriving in time to see Katerina or Tomas.

He called his police friend, Rafael, asking for help in finding Katerina's address back in Cambridge. Rafael called him back within twenty minutes with the address. At least that was one problem solved.

With a heavy sigh he crossed over to his own gate and settled into one of the uncomfortable plastic chairs. He wished more than ever that he'd spent more time talking to Katerina last night, rather than making love. Not that he regretted that part. He just wished they would have talked first.

He could only hope she would be willing to listen, to give him another chance, once he arrived in the U.S.

Nineteen and a half hours later Kat, Tommy and Juliet finally arrived home. Diana had gone to her own apartment and Kat couldn't blame her friend for wanting to sleep in her own bed.

Kat was exhausted, but she was far more worried about her sister. Juliet's pain had gotten worse the more they'd moved, and changing planes and then taking a train back to Cambridge had obviously been too much for her.

She was tempted to take Juliet straight to the hospital, but since the time was close to midnight, she decided against it. Rest would be the best thing for her sister, so she helped Juliet get into bed before giving her more pain medication. She'd have to arrange for follow-up doctor's appointments in the morning.

Unfortunately, Tommy wasn't nearly as tired. Just like on the way over to Spain, he'd slept on the plane and she wanted to burst into tears when he started bouncing on his bed.

After several minutes of fighting she gave up. "Okay, fine, let's go downstairs and watch a movie."

She put in a DVD and stretched out on the couch, holding her son in front of her, determined to get in at least a short nap. With any luck, Tommy would be tired enough to sleep after the movie was over.

Between Tommy's messed-up sleep cycle and her sister's pain, Kat only managed to get about four hours of sleep. Not nearly enough, but she would just have to make do. After making breakfast and encouraging Juliet to eat, she spent a good hour on the phone, making arrangements for Juliet to be seen by a doctor who specialized in head injuries.

Her sister was still slightly confused, but she was certainly better than she'd been when the breathing tube had been removed. At least she wasn't asking about their mother any more.

There was a loud knock at her front door at ten-thirty in the morning, and Kat fully expected to see her friend Diana had returned.

When she saw Miguel standing there, she stared in shock, wondering if her eyes were playing tricks on her. She blinked, but he didn't vanish. As she stared at him, she realized he looked as disheveled as she felt, indicating he must have been traveling all night. On one level she was glad to see him, but at the same time his timing couldn't have been worse.

"Miguel? How did you find me?" She didn't mean to sound ungracious, but lack of sleep made it difficult to think clearly. She was shocked to see him, but she couldn't deny she felt a warm glow at the knowledge that he'd come all this way to find her.

"I just missed you at Seville airport. I'm sorry we didn't get a chance to talk before you had to leave." He stared at her for a long moment as if trying to gauge her reaction. "May I come in?"

She smiled, although her eyes were gritty with lack of sleep. "Sure, but unfortunately, we're just getting ready to leave. Juliet has a doctor's appointment with a neurologist at Cambridge University Hospital." She stepped back, allowing him to come into her home. She frowned when she realized he didn't have so much as a suitcase with him.

For a moment her tired brain cells couldn't make sense of it all. Was Miguel planning to stay here with her? No, it made more sense that he must have left his luggage back in his hotel room.

"I think that is a good idea," Miguel was saying. "The doctors there will make sure she's really okay. Is she still confused?"

"A little. Not as bad as before, though."

"She probably just needs a little time." Miguel fell

silent and she wondered what he was thinking as he glanced around her small home. After her mother had died, she had taken over the house payments and promised Juliet her half when she graduated from college.

"Maybe we can get together later on?" she suggested, glancing at the clock. If they didn't leave soon, they'd be late.

"I could stay here with Tomas, if you think that would help," Miguel offered.

She opened her mouth to refuse, even though going to the doctor's appointment would be much easier without dragging Tommy along. Tommy had only met Miguel twice and she couldn't bear to leave him with someone he probably still considered a stranger. "I don't know if that's such a good idea," she said slowly.

Glancing over her shoulder, she noticed Tommy hovering in the kitchen doorway, staring at Miguel with wide eyes. He wasn't crying, but he wasn't rushing over to greet Miguel either.

"Please?" Miguel asked. "I think he'll be fine. He doesn't seem afraid of me."

"Tommy, do you remember Mr. Vasquez?" she asked.

Tommy nodded, sticking his thumb in his mouth, something he only did when he was really tired. And suddenly, knowing that Tommy would probably fall asleep sooner than later, she made up her mind to take Miguel up on his offer.

"All right, you can stay here with Tommy. I would suggest you put a movie on for him as he's probably going to fall asleep soon. His days and nights are a little mixed up from the flight home."

Miguel's smile warmed her down to her toes. "I think I can manage that."

She forced herself to look away, trying not to think about the fact that Miguel was here for his son first and foremost. Obviously, Miguel wanted more time to get to know his son. But she couldn't help feeling a pang of resentment that Miguel was acting as if the night they'd spent together hadn't happened. "All right, we'll be back in a couple of hours."

Miguel helped her get Juliet out to the car, before going back inside. Leaving him in her house felt weird, but she kept her attention focused on her sister.

She could only manage one crisis at a time.

Kat was thrilled when Dr. Sandlow announced that Juliet's head injury seemed to be resolving without a problem. After a long exam, blood work and a follow-up CT scan of her head, he'd decided Juliet was stable enough not to be admitted. "I'd like to see her back in a week," he said. "And she also needs to start attending physical therapy three days a week."

She tried not to wince, wondering how in the world she'd be able to return to work while taking Juliet to therapy three days a week. She still had at least another week of vacation time saved up, but after that was gone, she'd need to apply for a leave of absence.

Time to worry more about that later.

The appointment had lasted longer than she'd anticipated, which was fine, except that they'd missed lunch. She stopped on the way home and picked up a bucket of fried chicken, mashed potatoes and coleslaw in case Miguel and Tommy were hungry too.

She parked her car in the driveway, rather than pulling into the garage, so that it was easier to maneuver Juliet out of the front passenger seat. She was somewhat surprised that Miguel didn't come out to help as she hooked her arms under Juliet's armpits to help her stand.

"Are you okay?" Kat asked, as she grabbed the crutches from where she'd propped them against the door.

"Fine," Juliet murmured, although her upper lip was beaded with sweat.

"Just a few more feet and you can rest, okay?" Moving around was obviously good for Juliet, but it was almost time for more pain medication. The way Juliet winced and groaned with every single swing of the crutches made Kat feel bad.

They managed to get into the house without incident and she immediately steered her sister towards the guest bedroom. Once Juliet was settled, she went back out to the main living area to look for Miguel and Tommy.

She found them on the sofa in the living room, both of them asleep. Miguel held Tommy close against his chest.

She stared at the two of them, father and son, feeling abruptly alone. The two had bonded while she'd been gone and Tommy clearly needed his father the same way Miguel needed him. She should be thrilled that they were together at last.

But she couldn't shake the sense of desolation. All this time she'd told herself she wanted a family. But she'd had a family, with Tommy and Juliet.

Now she was forced to realize what she really wanted was for Miguel to love her as much as she loved him.

But did Miguel have the capability of loving her the way she wanted him to? Would he stick by her and Tommy not just in the good times but through the bad times as well?

Or would he leave the minute things got rough, just like her father?

## CHAPTER FOURTEEN

MIGUEL felt a soft weight being lifted off his chest, and his arms tightened, instinctively holding on. He forced his eyes open and found Katerina leaning over him, her exquisite green eyes snapping with fury.

Confused, he tried to comprehend what he'd done to upset her. For a moment he didn't even remember he was in the U.S., until he glanced down to see Tomas was fast asleep on his chest. Abruptly all the memories tumbled to the surface.

"Let him go, Miguel. I need to put him down in his bed," Katerina said curtly. Still foggy with exhaustion, he released his hold so that she could lift their son into her arms. He instantly missed the warmth radiating from Tomas' soft body.

She disappeared from the living room and he used the few moments alone to pull himself together. How long had he been asleep? He couldn't remember.

With a guilty glance at the clock, he knew he'd slept longer than he should have. A part of him was disgusted that he'd wasted a good hour sleeping when he could have been making up for lost time with his son.

Although they would have plenty of time to get to know each other. Wouldn't they? On the long flight to the U.S. he'd finally realized that where he and Katerina lived wasn't important. Being together was all that mattered.

He kept waiting for the reality of his decision to sink in, but he didn't have the itchy feeling of wanting to leave. Was it possible that joining Doctors Without Borders really wasn't his dream?

Had it just been a way to escape?

He frowned and stretched in an effort to shake off his deep thoughts. Lifting his head, the distinct scent of fried chicken made him realize how hungry he was. He followed his nose into the kitchen.

There were bags of food lying haphazardly on the table, as if they'd been set down in a hurry. Before he could reach for one, Katerina returned.

"Tommy will be down soon, he wouldn't go back to sleep." Her slightly accusing gaze made him wonder if she believed that was his fault. Maybe it was. "We'll have lunch and then you'll need to leave, Miguel. I can't deal with you right now. I have Tommy and Juliet to care for."

He wanted to argue, but the lines of fatigue on her face tugged at his heart. She looked so exhausted he wanted to sweep her up and take her to bed. But, of course, he couldn't.

Somehow he'd thought she'd be happy to see him. But so far she'd seemed more annoyed. Had he misunderstood her feelings towards him? His heart squeezed in his chest.

He told himself to have patience, even though it wasn't easy. Tomas came running into the room and he helped Katerina pull out the fried chicken, mashed potatoes and coleslaw. He noticed that she made sure Tomas had some food on his plate and that she made a plate for her sister, before worrying about eating anything herself.

"I'll be right back," she murmured, taking the food down the hall towards a small bedroom. He felt guilty all over again, knowing that Katerina had managed to get Juliet inside without his assistance.

He watched Tomas eat, determined to wait for Katerina. She returned quickly enough, dropping into a chair across from him.

"How is she?" he asked.

"Sleeping. Dr. Sandlow said she's fine, though. She needs to start physical therapy three times a week. I'll help her with her lunch later." She took a healthy bite of her chicken, and then seemed to notice he hadn't eaten. "Don't you like fried chicken?" she asked.

"Of course. Who doesn't?" He flashed a reassuring smile before turning his attention to his own plate. He wanted to help her, but sensed he was treading on thin ice. For some reason, she'd been angry with him for falling asleep. Either because she thought he'd put Tomas in danger, or because he'd slept when she couldn't. Or maybe because he'd made himself at home. Regardless, he knew he could help ease her burden by staying, if she'd let him.

"Lean over your plate, Tommy," she said gently when pieces of fried chicken dropped from his mouth and hit the floor. "Don't make a mess."

"No mess," Tomas said with his mouth full.

"Is the shopping mall still located a few miles from

the hospital?" he asked. "I need to purchase clothes and toiletries."

She frowned. "Did the airline lose your luggage?"

"No. I didn't bring anything except my passport. I was racing to catch up with you and Tomas. As you'd already boarded the plane, they wouldn't let me talk to you. I ended up going through London to get here."

She looked shocked to hear he'd followed her. After several long moments she finished her meal and sat back in her chair. "Yes," she murmured. "The shopping mall is still there."

"Katerina, we need to talk." He glanced at Tomas, who was starting to wiggle around in his booster chair. He was tempted to smile at how their son had smeared mashed potatoes and gravy all over himself.

"Not now. As I said, I have other things to worry about at the moment. Tommy needs a bath and then I need to care for my sister. I'm sorry, but I'm afraid you'll have to wait until I get things caught up around here." She stood and picked up Tommy. "Goodbye, Miguel."

She turned and left, no doubt intending to give Tomas a bath. He wanted nothing more than to help, but she'd made her wishes very clear.

With a sigh he pushed away from the table and began clearing the dirty dishes, storing the leftovers in the fridge. Maybe she wanted him gone, but he wasn't about to leave this mess for her. Not when she looked like she was dead on her feet.

He wanted to believe that Katerina was just tired and jet-lagged, that she didn't mean what she'd said.

But since he'd arrived, she hadn't given any indication of wanting to pick up their relationship where they'd left off. If not for his brother going missing, they would have had time to talk. To plan. Surely there was a way to make this work? Surely Katerina felt something for him?

So why was he feeling as if she wished he hadn't come to the U.S.?

As he washed and dried the dishes, he racked his brain for a way to bridge the gap that had somehow widened between them.

Because if she thought he was giving up that easily, she was dead wrong.

Kat ran warm water and bubble bath into the tub for Tommy, knowing she'd been unfair to Miguel. He'd come all this way, had actually followed her to the airport in Seville, flying all night, only to have her demand that he leave. She hadn't even asked about Luis.

She set Tommy into the tub, kneeling alongside to keep a close eye on him. Tommy played in the water, splashing bubbles everywhere. She was so exhausted, so emotionally drained that she didn't even notice bubbles had landed on her hair.

She'd been badly shaken by the sight of Miguel holding Tommy, both of them looking adorable as they'd slept. She was a terrible mother to be jealous, even for an instant, of her son's love for his father. And the sad truth was that Tommy didn't even know that Miguel was his father yet.

But he would, soon.

For a moment she rested her forehead on the smooth, cool porcelain of the tub. She should be glad Miguel wanted to be a part of Tommy's life. She should be glad that he'd come here to Cambridge, rather than asking her to consider moving to Seville.

Yet, she couldn't help wishing that they would have time alone, to explore the passion that simmered between them. She knew Miguel wanted her, but she didn't know if there was any way he'd ever come to love her. She felt confused and exhausted.

She had her sister to care for, and Tommy too. And soon she'd have to go back to work. There wouldn't be time for her and Miguel to renew their relationship. But there would be plenty of time for him to establish a relationship with his son.

She lifted her head, instantly ashamed of herself for being selfish. Her son was what mattered, not her own ridiculous feelings. Giving her head a shake to clear the troublesome thoughts, she quickly washed Tommy's hair and then pulled him out of the water, engulfing his slippery body in a thick, fluffy towel.

After getting Tommy dressed in clean clothes, and straightening out her own disheveled appearance, she went back out to the kitchen, half-afraid Miguel would still be there. He wasn't, but she was pleasantly surprised to find her kitchen was spotless, every bit of mess cleaned up, including the floor around Tommy's booster chair.

His kind thoughtfulness only made her feel more miserable for her earlier abruptness. Was it too late to catch up to him? She almost headed for the door when she heard thumping noises coming from Juliet's room. Juliet was up, trying to navigate with her crutches, leaving her no choice but to hurry down to help her sister.

Forcing her to push thoughts of Miguel firmly out of her mind.

An entire twenty-four hours went by without any word or visit from Miguel. Kat should have been relieved to have one less thing to deal with, but instead she was on edge. Had something happened to him? Had he decided she was too much of a witch to deal with? Had he decided to return to Spain after all?

She still didn't know his phone number, or if his cellphone from Spain would even work here in the U.S. She felt much better after getting a good night's sleep and was pleased to note that Juliet was also doing better every day.

Getting her sister to therapy wasn't too bad, especially as Juliet insisted on doing things for herself. There was a truce between them, a closeness that hadn't been there before Juliet had left to study abroad. Kat hoped that this terrible accident would bring them closer together.

"Where's that Spanish doctor?" Juliet asked, when they'd returned from therapy.

Kat shrugged. "I'm not sure. Why?"

"Come on, sis, you're not fooling me. He's obviously Tommy's father. And you love him, don't you?"

She wanted to protest, but really what was the point? "My feelings don't matter as he doesn't feel the same way."

Juliet stared at her for a long moment. "You never

asked me what happened. I mean, how I ended up getting hit by a car."

Kat pulled up a chair to sit beside her sister's bed. "Jules, you were in the I.C.U. on a ventilator when I came to visit. And by the time you'd recovered, you were confused and told me you couldn't remember. Has that changed? Do you remember what happened?"

Juliet took a deep breath and let it out slowly. "I fell in love with a guy named Enrique. He was much older and so mature. I never told him how I felt, but I thought we had this great connection. Until I found him with another woman."

Kat sucked in a harsh breath. After having both of their fathers leave their mother, she knew that would be the worst betrayal of all. "Oh, Jules…"

"I was so upset I started crying and ran into the road." Juliet shrugged. "Thankfully, I don't remember much after that."

"I'm so sorry." Kat reached out and took her sister's hand. "I'm sure that was really difficult for you to see him with someone else."

"Yes, it was. After the way my dad left, I spend half my time waiting for the guy I'm dating to show his true colors. But now I wonder if I just liked Enrique because he was safe. I think I've been avoiding relationships, Kat. Because of our fathers."

Kat tried to follow her sister's logic. "But you just said you fell for Enrique. Wasn't that a relationship?"

"Not really. He was older and friendly with me. But it wasn't like we even kissed or anything. There was another guy who liked me, who was closer to my age, but I avoided him. I told myself it was because I liked

Enrique, but the truth of the matter was that I was avoiding being hurt." Juliet tightened her grip around Kat's fingers. "Don't do that, Kat. Don't avoid Miguel because you don't want to get hurt."

Juliet's words struck a chord deep inside. For someone so much younger, Juliet had great insight. "It's more complicated than that, Jules. He's Tommy's father. We have to get along, for his sake."

"Tell him how you feel," Juliet insisted. "Don't let your pride or fear get in the way."

Was her sister right? Had she avoided talking on a personal level with Miguel because she was afraid of being hurt? They'd never really talked about their joint custody arrangement because she'd avoided the topic. The realization made her wince.

Maybe her sister was right. "Get some rest Jules, okay?" she said, changing the subject. "We'll eat around six o'clock. I have a pot roast in the slow cooker for dinner."

"Okay," Juliet murmured, closing her eyes.

Kat left her sister's room to head for the kitchen. She was surprised to hear the sound of voices.

"Meegl," Tommy shouted and it took her a minute to figure out that it was a mangled version of Miguel.

"Tomas!" Miguel responded, and she entered the kitchen in time to see her son launch himself at his father. Miguel laughed and clasped Tommy close, looking dangerously attractive wearing casual clothes, jeans and a long-sleeved denim shirt. "I've missed you," he said, nuzzling Tommy's neck.

"Me too," her son said, hugging him.

For a moment, seeing the two of them together, father

and son, made her want to cry. But then Miguel lifted his head and caught her gaze, with such intensity she could barely breathe. "Hi, Miguel," she said inanely.

"Katerina," he murmured, and for a moment she thought she saw frank desire in his gaze, before he bent over to set Tommy back on his feet. "Would you allow me to take you out for dinner this evening?"

"I'm sorry, I would but I don't have a babysitter," she said, tearing her gaze from his. She figured that he wanted to finalize their co-custody agreement and was determined not to continue avoiding the topic. Thankfully, she felt better prepared now after a good night's sleep. She forced a smile. "I have a pot roast in the slow cooker if you want to stay."

"Diana said she'd come over to babysit. And she's more than capable of watching over Juliet as well." He took a step toward her, holding out his hand. "Please?"

He'd called Diana? She could hardly hide her surprise. And now that he'd taken that excuse away, she couldn't think of a reason to refuse. "All right," she agreed. "But I need some time to change."

"I'll wait," he said.

The next few hours flew by as she showered, changed and then greeted Diana, who seemed glad to be back on American soil. As Miguel held the door of his rental car open for her, she felt a bit like a girl going out on her first date.

"Are you sure you know how to drive?" she asked, as he slid behind the wheel. "Maybe you should have brought Fernando here with you."

His teeth flashed in a broad smile. "Fernando is taking over the Vasquez olive farm. Believe it or not, my brother Luis has decided he wants to build things, instead of being a farmer."

"So he's okay, then?" she asked. "You found him all right?"

"He's fine. He was afraid to tell me how much he hated the farm." For a moment a dark shadow crossed his face, but then it was gone. "I'm convinced he's going to be fine now that he's following his dream."

Dread knotted her stomach, and she had the most insane feeling he was about to tell her he was going to follow his own dream. His dream of joining Doctors Without Borders. "I'm glad," she said in a choked tone.

He slanted a glance in her direction as he pulled into the driveway of a well-known hotel located mere blocks from her house. "I hope you don't mind if we have a quiet dinner here?"

"Of course not."

He led the way inside to the fancy restaurant located just off the hotel lobby. There weren't too many people dining, but it didn't matter as they were led to a small quiet table in the back.

Miguel treated her courteously, holding her chair for her and then asking what she'd like to drink. They started with a light appetizer and a bottle of Shiraz.

"Katerina," he said, reaching over to take her hand. "I have something very important to ask you."

She felt surprisingly calm, despite knowing they were about to settle their future joint custody arrangement once and for all. Her sister's advice echoed in her mind.

"Yes, Miguel?" She took a sip of her wine and carefully set it down.

In a flash he was out of his seat and kneeling in front of her chair. She stared at him in shock when he flipped open a small black velvet ring box, revealing a large diamond ring. "Katerina, will you marry me?"

For a moment her heart soared and she wanted to shout yes at the top of her lungs.

Except he hadn't said anything about love.

"Miguel, we don't have to get married," she said, tearing her gaze away and wishing she'd ordered something stronger than wine. "We'll work something out so that we'll both be actively involved in Tommy's life. I'll even consider moving to Seville, after Juliet is better, if that's what you want. You don't have to do this."

He never moved, still kneeling before her, his gaze steadily holding hers. "Katerina, I love you. I was foolish to leave you four and a half years ago. I let my mother's bitterness affect my outlook on life. It's true that I want to be a part of my son's life, but that's not why I'm asking you to marry me. I'm asking because I can't imagine my life without you."

She felt her jaw drop open in shocked surprise. She wanted so badly to believe him. Trusting men wasn't easy for her, but wasn't this what she'd secretly wanted? She couldn't allow her mother's tragic life to affect her ability to find happiness.

"Miguel, are you sure? Because there's no rush. Besides, I thought you always wanted to work with Doctors Without Borders? I don't want you resent us at some future point because you didn't get to follow your dream."

"My dream isn't to join Doctors Without Borders any more," he said. "It pains me to say this, but I realize now I've been partly using that dream to avoid getting close to anyone. Until I met you. I've fallen in love with you, Katerina. And I don't care where we live, here or Seville, it doesn't matter. Nothing matters except you and our son. And any other children we decide to have."

He loved her? She wanted so badly to believe him. Her small sliver of doubt faded when she saw the pure emotion shining from his dark eyes. And somehow she managed to find the courage to open her heart to him. "Yes, Miguel," she murmured huskily. "I will marry you. Because I love you, too. And I can't imagine my life without you either." She felt wonderful saying the words, knowing deep in her heart that they were true.

"*Te amo,* Katerina," he murmured, taking out the ring and slowly sliding the band over the fourth finger of her left hand. She barely had time to enjoy the sparkle when he stood and then drew her to her feet before pulling her gently into his arms. He kissed her, gently at first and then with such passion she almost forgot they weren't alone.

He gently pulled back, simply staring down at her for a long moment. "I love you, so much, Katerina," he whispered. "I promise to show you just how much I love you every day for the rest of our lives."

"I love you, too, Miguel." She lifted up on tiptoe to kiss him again, ignoring the waiters and waitresses clapping in the background. "And I want Tommy to have at least one brother and one sister."

He laughed. "Anything you say," he agreed huskily, before kissing her again.

As she clung to his shoulders, reveling in the kiss, she realized that with a little faith and love...dreams really could come true.

# EPILOGUE

MIGUEL was pleased and humbled that Katerina had wanted to be married in Seville. He stood at the front of the church, amazed at how crowded it was. Apparently everyone in Seville wanted to be there to share in their wedding. Juliet was there too, standing as Katerina's maid of honor. She was fully recovered now from her accident and was determined to finish her semester abroad. His brother Luis hadn't touched a drop of alcohol since selling the farm, and he stood straight and tall next to Miguel as his best man.

There were many friends and family in the church, some even having come all the way from the U.S. to be there. And he couldn't help smiling when he saw Pedro sitting near the front, wearing his Sunday best, craning his neck to get a glimpse of the bride.

When the music began, the first one to walk down the aisle was Tomas. Miguel grinned when his son walked slowly as if afraid he might drop the small satin pillow holding their wedding bands. When Tomas reached the front of the church, Luis stepped forward and took the rings. Miguel put a hand on his son's shoulder, keeping him at his side.

"Hi, Daddy," Tomas said in a loud whisper. "I didn't drop them."

"Good boy," he whispered back.

Juliet was next, walking with only the slightest bit of a limp, hardly noticeable to anyone except him.

And then Katerina stepped forward, so beautiful his chest ached. The entire church went silent with awe, but when she caught his gaze and smiled, the love shining from her eyes made him catch his breath. He forced himself to stay right where he was when he wanted very badly to rush forward to greet her.

They had two priests, one who spoke English for Katerina, even though she was already broadening her knowledge of the Spanish language.

"Mama's beautiful, isn't she?" Tomas said again, in a loud whisper.

"Very beautiful," Miguel agreed. "Be quiet now, Tomas, okay?"

"Okay," he agreed, nodding vigorously. When Katerina reached his side, he took her hand in his and together they turned to face the two priests.

As anxious he was to have Katerina become his wife, he planned to enjoy every moment of this day, the first day of their new life, together.

\* \* \* \* \*

# ROMANCE

| | |
|---|---|
| **A Ring to Secure His Heir** | Lynne Graham |
| **What His Money Can't Hide** | Maggie Cox |
| **Woman in a Sheikh's World** | Sarah Morgan |
| **At Dante's Service** | Chantelle Shaw |
| **At His Majesty's Request** | Maisey Yates |
| **Breaking the Greek's Rules** | Anne McAllister |
| **The Ruthless Caleb Wilde** | Sandra Marton |
| **The Price of Success** | Maya Blake |
| **The Man From her Wayward Past** | Susan Stephens |
| **Blame it on the Bikini** | Natalie Anderson |
| **The English Lord's Secret Son** | Margaret Way |
| **The Secret That Changed Everything** | Lucy Gordon |
| **Baby Under the Christmas Tree** | Teresa Carpenter |
| **The Cattleman's Special Delivery** | Barbara Hannay |
| **Secrets of the Rich & Famous** | Charlotte Phillips |
| **Her Man In Manhattan** | Trish Wylie |
| **His Bride in Paradise** | Joanna Neil |
| **Christmas Where She Belongs** | Meredith Webber |

# MEDICAL

| | |
|---|---|
| **From Christmas to Eternity** | Caroline Anderson |
| **Her Little Spanish Secret** | Laura Iding |
| **Christmas with Dr Delicious** | Sue MacKay |
| **One Night That Changed Everything** | Tina Beckett |

*Mills & Boon® Large Print*

*December 2012*

# ROMANCE

| | |
|---|---|
| **Contract with Consequences** | Miranda Lee |
| **The Sheikh's Last Gamble** | Trish Morey |
| **The Man She Shouldn't Crave** | Lucy Ellis |
| **The Girl He'd Overlooked** | Cathy Williams |
| **Mr Right, Next Door!** | Barbara Wallace |
| **The Cowboy Comes Home** | Patricia Thayer |
| **The Rancher's Housekeeper** | Rebecca Winters |
| **Her Outback Rescuer** | Marion Lennox |
| **A Tainted Beauty** | Sharon Kendrick |
| **One Night With The Enemy** | Abby Green |
| **The Dangerous Jacob Wilde** | Sandra Marton |

# HISTORICAL

| | |
|---|---|
| **A Not So Respectable Gentleman?** | Diane Gaston |
| **Outrageous Confessions of Lady Deborah** | Marguerite Kaye |
| **His Unsuitable Viscountess** | Michelle Styles |
| **Lady with the Devil's Scar** | Sophia James |
| **Betrothed to the Barbarian** | Carol Townend |

# MEDICAL

| | |
|---|---|
| **Sydney Harbour Hospital: Bella's Wishlist** | Emily Forbes |
| **Doctor's Mile-High Fling** | Tina Beckett |
| **Hers For One Night Only?** | Carol Marinelli |
| **Unlocking the Surgeon's Heart** | Jessica Matthews |
| **Marriage Miracle in Swallowbrook** | Abigail Gordon |
| **Celebrity in Braxton Falls** | Judy Campbell |

# Mills & Boon® Hardback

## January 2013

# ROMANCE

| | |
|---|---|
| Beholden to the Throne | Carol Marinelli |
| The Petrelli Heir | Kim Lawrence |
| Her Little White Lie | Maisey Yates |
| Her Shameful Secret | Susanna Carr |
| The Incorrigible Playboy | Emma Darcy |
| No Longer Forbidden? | Dani Collins |
| The Enigmatic Greek | Catherine George |
| The Night That Started It All | Anna Cleary |
| The Secret Wedding Dress | Ally Blake |
| Driving Her Crazy | Amy Andrews |
| The Heir's Proposal | Raye Morgan |
| The Soldier's Sweetheart | Soraya Lane |
| The Billionaire's Fair Lady | Barbara Wallace |
| A Bride for the Maverick Millionaire | Marion Lennox |
| Take One Arranged Marriage... | Shoma Narayanan |
| Wild About the Man | Joss Wood |
| Breaking the Playboy's Rules | Emily Forbes |
| Hot-Shot Doc Comes to Town | Susan Carlisle |

# MEDICAL

| | |
|---|---|
| The Surgeon's Doorstep Baby | Marion Lennox |
| Dare She Dream of Forever? | Lucy Clark |
| Craving Her Soldier's Touch | Wendy S. Marcus |
| Secrets of a Shy Socialite | Wendy S. Marcus |

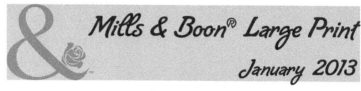

Mills & Boon® Large Print

January 2013

# ROMANCE

| | |
|---|---|
| **Unlocking her Innocence** | Lynne Graham |
| **Santiago's Command** | Kim Lawrence |
| **His Reputation Precedes Him** | Carole Mortimer |
| **The Price of Retribution** | Sara Craven |
| **The Valtieri Baby** | Caroline Anderson |
| **Slow Dance with the Sheriff** | Nikki Logan |
| **Bella's Impossible Boss** | Michelle Douglas |
| **The Tycoon's Secret Daughter** | Susan Meier |
| **Just One Last Night** | Helen Brooks |
| **The Greek's Acquisition** | Chantelle Shaw |
| **The Husband She Never Knew** | Kate Hewitt |

# HISTORICAL

| | |
|---|---|
| **His Mask of Retribution** | Margaret McPhee |
| **How to Disgrace a Lady** | Bronwyn Scott |
| **The Captain's Courtesan** | Lucy Ashford |
| **Man Behind the Façade** | June Francis |
| **The Highlander's Stolen Touch** | Terri Brisbin |

# MEDICAL

| | |
|---|---|
| **Sydney Harbour Hospital: Marco's Temptation** | Fiona McArthur |
| **Waking Up With His Runaway Bride** | Louisa George |
| **The Legendary Playboy Surgeon** | Alison Roberts |
| **Falling for Her Impossible Boss** | Alison Roberts |
| **Letting Go With Dr Rodriguez** | Fiona Lowe |
| **Dr Tall, Dark...and Dangerous?** | Lynne Marshall |